THE VISCOUNT'S JOURNEY

Viscount Garrett Rashley has six months to complete the terms of his late uncle's will to inherit Finchston Park. He must lose his freedom as a single man and marry Miriah Carrington, a charming but talkative young lady. Miriah is thrilled; this is the man she has waited for. But nothing hurts worse than to have the man of her dreams marry her out of duty. Miriah wants to be cherished for herself alone, so she sets out to win Garrett's true affections . . .

JO ANNE McCRAW

THE VISCOUNT'S JOURNEY

Complete and Unabridged

LINFORD
Leicester

First published in 2001 in the
United States of America

First Linford Edition
published 2003

Copyright © 2000 by Jo Anne McCraw

British Library CIP Data

McCraw, Jo Anne
    The Viscount's journey.—Large print ed.—
Linford romance library
1. Love stories
2. Large type books
I. Title
813.6 [F]

ISBN 1–8439–5090–1

Published by
F. A. Thorpe (Publishing)
Anstey, Leicestershire

Set by Words & Graphics Ltd.
Anstey, Leicestershire
Printed and bound in Great Britain by
T. J. International Ltd., Padstow, Cornwall

This book is printed on acid-free paper

For Heidi, my fur child and muse
who is in doggy heaven,
I miss you so much!

For my hard working, yet 'let's
meet at the tea room' critique
group: Nancy Madison and Chris
McKeever, and I can't leave out
Laura Krause who was
instrumental in the group in its
inception five years ago.

For my mentor: Pat Cody who has
taught me so much about research,
revising, and writing; we enjoyed
the Rose Garden Tea Room
a few times ourselves.

For my family and friends who had
faith in me, my most sincere
thanks, and I love you all!

1

May 1815, Guildford, England

'Beg pardon, Mr. Peabody. You say I have to marry Miss Miriah Carrington before I gain the inheritance?' Lord Garrett William Rashley clutched the arms of the leather-bound chair and glared at the gray-haired fellow sitting behind the massive mahogany desk. 'Why?'

'Simply because your uncle wished it, or he would not have stipulated such a measure.' The solicitor pushed back the glasses slipping down his narrow nose. 'He paid me handsomely to carry out his orders, and I shall. Remember, you have until November, my lord. If you fail to marry, the inheritance will go to your younger cousin.'

Gathering his papers, the solicitor stuffed them into his leather satchel and pulled his short, bony frame from the massive chair that dwarfed him. He bowed then shuffled across the carpeted floor and quit the room.

Garrett propelled himself out of the chair and stalked to the tall window that overlooked the grounds at Rashley Hall. A sparrowhawk swooshed by and flapped its short, rounded wings. The dashing gray bird keck-keck-kecked as it taunted Garrett with its freedom. Less than six months of independence was all he had left.

'Uncle Charles knew my feelings about matrimony, since the day Dorothea left me at the altar. Why would he do such a despicable thing, forcing me into a life I cannot abide?' Garrett ran his fingers through his hair and glanced at his older half brother, Joseph, the Baron Rashley, clad in a brown waistcoat and buff colored pantaloons. One of his knee-length booted legs rested over the other. 'He never married, yet he expects it of me. It is hardly fair.'

'Perhaps your uncle was not happy in his bachelor state. Maybe he didn't want you to be lonely in that huge house.' Joseph pulled his tall frame out of the high, wing-backed chair and laughed. 'After all, you do enjoy our children. And it's plain to see that your Uncle Charles expects you to produce an heir for the estate.'

'Stuff and nonsense, Joseph.' Garrett paced across the worn carpeted floor. 'Why couldn't he have willed the estate over without strings attached? You are lucky that Rashley Hall was entailed to you by our father. No stipulations there.'

'Matters are not always as easy for a second son. You are fortunate that you were your mother's brother's favorite nephew, or another of your male cousins would have inherited. One of them still may if you do not marry. You cannot let that happen. No one is as fond of Finchston Park as you.'

Joseph was right. He did care for Finchston Park. He also shared his

3

uncle's love for hunting and fishing. Uncle Charles had treated him as the son he'd never had. Garrett had admired him for his patience with him after Garrett's mother left them. No one had to tell him that he was a trying child during that period. Besides, he loved his uncle. Rather than admitting those facts, he said. 'Thank you for heaping guilt on me, Joseph.'

'What's a half brother for if he cannot make one feel low?' Joseph winked at him.

He smiled at Joseph, who at thirty-three was older by five years. 'And now, you tease me.' Garrett had to admit that he was a little envious of his half-sibling, not for having inherited the title from their father, but for having found the perfect wife. Garrett made his mistake in putting his hopes in Dorothea. But she failed him.

'You take matters too seriously, Gar. Perhaps this Miss Carrington possesses a fine sense of humor, and that is why Uncle chose her for you.'

'Whatever his reason, why did he not tell me before he put it in writing? That baffles me no end.' Garrett plopped down in the chair causing the leather to squeak. Uncle knew the misery Garrett endured after his failed engagement, not to mention the previous pain of his mother's abandonment when he was a child. He didn't trust his judgement in women enough to risk his freedom.

'Are you jealous that you were not the firstborn son?'

'Of course not, Joseph. And I do not hold you responsible for my lot in life. In fact, I admire you for the way you have run Rashley Hall since Father's death eleven years ago. You carry responsibility well. My heart would not be in it as yours is. My association with the place is tainted by unpleasant memories.' He frowned. 'I do not understand how Father could stand the place after Mother left.'

'He forgave her long ago. No good comes out of harboring grudges and past hurts. You must move forward,

Gar. Nothing will change the past. I married. Look at Jennifer. She has not left me, nor will she do so. Why can you not trust a lady? Abigail has been more of a mother to you than a half sister. All ladies are not like your mother.'

'You're forgetting my botched engagement to Dorothea Haversham. She didn't have the audacity to show up at our wedding.' Years and hard-learned wisdom enabled him to build a wall around his pride and no lady would cross that barrier.

'Gar. The two of you were mismatched from the beginning. Jen and I both concurred that Dorothea used you to make that fellow Cheetham jealous and it worked. Be thankful she did not go through with the ceremony.'

'You are correct on that account.' Garrett sighed. 'From that very day the thought of marriage has never entered my mind.' Nor did responsibility until now. He'd never dreamed he would have the chance to own Finchston Hall.

'Perhaps your Uncle Charles thought

he could do better in choosing a bride for you. He knew you wouldn't take a wife after Dorothea unless one was forced upon you.' Joseph quickly amended his statement. 'Forced is doing it a bit too brown . . . '

'I believe your choice of word is most appropriate. He did this on purpose to settle me down. Hunting and gaming was not what he wished me to do with my life after the Peninsular War, and I very well know it.' Garrett drew in a deep breath. The scent of old tobacco reminded him of the long hours his Father sat closeted in this room working figures and reading. Now the walls were closing in.

'Gar, may I inquire if you know the lady in question?'

'Yes, I did chance to meet her over four years ago. If I remember correctly, she was thin and quite small . . . with blond hair and blue eyes. At least I think they were blue. I danced with her once or twice at different functions. Come to think of it, there were two sisters, and I'm not sure which one was Miss Miriah.' He put his fist to his lips, rested his elbow on the arm of the chair and tried to visualize the girl.

'Well now, what do you propose to do, Gar?'

'The only thing I can do if I want the inheritance.'

'Indeed. You should visit the estate. It may fill you with a sense of pride merely by being there. That is, if returning to London for the remainder of the season matters not to you?' Joseph came to stand beside Garrett's chair. 'And it certainly would give you the opportunity to call on Miss Carrington while you are in the neighborhood.'

'By all means. I must rush to her door.' Garrett spoke in a sarcastic tone. He hated being pushed into this arrangement, and the shortness of time only heightened his sense of losing his freedom. No longer was he in control of his life.

'With the title the Regent bestowed

upon you for your chivalrous service during the siege at Badajoz, you have become a prize catch in the eyes of many a young maiden and her mama. You, my little half brother, have a title after all.' A deep laugh rolled from Joseph's throat. Garrett shot a menacing glance at him.

'As if a title is what I have coveted all these years. And what do you mean by 'little'? We are at of the same height with one another.' He stood and leveled a look at Joseph.

'I meant it metaphorically, of course.'

'Indeed,' Garrett muttered as he took a turn about the room, pondering the land that held more appeal than the title he had acquired. 'You know Joseph, the land and the money will come in handy to support me. I may not have to turn to the East India Company for a living after all.'

Garrett flicked a piece of lint off the back of a stuffed chair. 'I believe I shall ride out on the morrow and pay a call on the Carringtons. There is nothing else I can do to own land except through an inheritance such as this, is there?' Garrett turned his gaze outside to the hedgerow of cherry-plum trees across from the library window. He had helped his father's gardener plant the small saplings the spring of his eighth birthday, a year after his mother left.

How could a mother leave her only child? He ran his fingers through his hair. Was Dorothea so much like his mother that she would have done the same had they married?

'I am always here to give you counsel if you need to talk.' Joseph slapped him lightly on the shoulder as he came to stand beside him.

Garrett glanced at him and saw the similarity between his half brother and himself. Their golden-brown hair and light blue eyes came from their father. At least he didn't look into the mirror and see much of his mother staring back at him.

His thoughts came back to earth as Joseph added. 'Of course, you could always turn to prayer.'

'Don't start with me on that subject. You know I attended services with you and Abigail when I was younger. I prayed every day for Mother to return home. God didn't answer my prayers. Then I was left at the altar two years ago.' He ground the words out harshly, and turned on his half brother. 'Where was God then, Joseph? He wasn't there!'

Joseph bowed his head.

'You don't understand how faith works, Garrett.'

'Really. Sometime you must astonish me with how it does work.' Garrett turned and marched out of the library. Pain burned into the core of his heart. Doubts replaced the faith he had been raised to believe in as a child. And what faith he had deserted him at the altar of St. Mary's Church. He slammed the door behind him as if to wake the dead.

★ ★ ★

Garrett reached Finchston Park before the dark of the late May sky overtook him. As he inhaled deeply, it amazed him that he could never get enough of the fresh clean air of England since the war. Birds trilled from the branches of the oak trees, and leaves rustled in the brisk breeze.

He surveyed his surroundings to get an idea of his holdings. Deer grazed on an adjacent carpet of grass in a park-like setting. From what he could see of the grasslands and apple orchards, the steward maintained the grounds and the Palladian house in satisfactory fashion. Sunlight glanced off the pale Bath stone of the impressive structure. The site was spectacular. It was easy to see why his uncle had such pride in his grand home.

'Danté, this will be all ours when I marry,' he told his horse. Looking at the house, he imagined himself standing at the head of the stairs, a blond lady at his side. The image of his father and mother came to mind, and he shook his head to erase the memory. At the sound of hooves kicking pebbles, he turned and forced a smile as his former military batman, Isaac Denby pulled up beside him. 'How does the place look to you, old man?'

'A fine looking estate, Garrett. I mean, my lord. I must start calling you proper-like before I join the other servants in that magnificent house as your valet.' The wiry man nodded toward the manor below the rise.

'I suppose you must, but in private you have my permission to call me whatever you wish. You earned that right by serving me in the war.' Giving the big chestnut Thoroughbred a pat on the neck. Garrett nudged him onward down the slope leading toward the front entrance.

A footman emerged from the servant's doorway below the outside entrance and took the horses' reins.

The stone-faced butler came down from the portico on one side of the double crab-pincer staircase and greeted them in a regal manner. 'Good afternoon, my lord.'

'Good afternoon, Hopson.' Nodding toward Isaac, he added, 'This is Isaac Denby, my valet. Are our rooms ready?'

'Yes, My lord. We prepared them after we received your missive yesterday. Dinner will be served at your convenience.'

'What is the usual time for dinner here?'

'Six of the clock, my lord.'

'Then I shall be down for dinner at the appointed time. I prefer, Hopson, to adapt to my surroundings as opposed to having them adapt to me.' Garrett mounted the steps, followed by Isaac. At the top of the stone staircase a footman held open the massive front door.

This house and its land represented the end to the carefree life Garrett lived. For the first time, responsibility filled him with a sense of pride in the legacy his uncle had left him. Joseph had been right on that matter.

Garrett stepped into the foyer and glanced around at the Roman interior. It was a bit too ornate for his taste, but he presumed that could change with a lady's touch and a few of his own ideas sprinkled in. Roman statues had never appealed to him, outside of a museum. The scent of fresh-cut flowers filled the high-ceilinged hall. The housekeeper had done a marvelous job in preparing the place on such short notice. Holland covers had most likely hung over the furnishings since Uncle's death, until yesterday that is.

Upon entering his suite, he inhaled the sweet scent of roses. He didn't care for flowers in his room, but he suspected that the fragrance was to cover the musty smell of rooms left vacant for too long a time. After all, Uncle had been ill for the past eighteen months and had not entertained guests for a couple of years before that.

'Isaac, please find another location for the vase of flowers by the bed. Preferably not in this room. I cannot sleep with so much fragrance nearby.'

'Aye, my lord.' His valet removed the vase.

★ ★ ★

After a night of tossing and turning, Garrett awoke at first light. Too many uncertainties kept his mind occupied. For one, what would he have to say to Miss Carrington after reappearing in her life? What if she was besotted with another? He could not marry her if her heart was otherwise engaged. He'd been through that once before.

Isaac came into the room and blinked. No doubt, he was surprised to find his master already out of bed and washing his face. 'I did not expect you up and about so early, sir.'

'I couldn't sleep.' Garrett dried his face with a soft cloth, adding, 'Fetch my riding coat and top boots, will you please?'

The valet bowed and went to the clothespress as Garrett buttoned his shirt at the neck and tucked it into his trousers. Turning, he saw Isaac carrying a tan coat over his arm along with boots dangling from his hand.

The smell of an early blooming honeysuckle hedge wafted through the open windows of the dining room. It reminded him of the many hours he spent bowling as a youth on these very grounds. After a cup of coffee, Garrett stepped out to the stable for a morning ride before breaking his fast.

Solitude helped him think. He needed to work out a plan of action. The day before leaving Rashley Hall, he had sent two letters. One went to Finchston Park, and the other to Mr. Carrington to inform him of his coming visit. A reply should arrive as soon as this morning.

Giving Danté his lead, he raced over the lush hillside. It was just as he remembered so long ago. Spring was a vista of beautiful colors. Everything appeared new and green. Perhaps this was a good omen. His life was changing. Could it be that it was budding anew, like the spring? Hope filled his heart for the first time in years. Perhaps Uncle Charles wanted his will to be a beginning for him. He hoped it was so.

The scent of chamomile growing wild in the field permeated the air, and a warm breeze blew against his face making him feel alive again. War had taken so much from him. Memories of a soldier falling with his horse and the scent of cannon fire mingled with death often haunted his nights. A new beginning, he thought with conviction in his heart. Yes, Uncle Charles had wanted that.

Garrett rode back to the stable. Dismounting, he gave Danté over to the head groom after rubbing the horse's neck. With lighter steps, he walked back to the house. Hopson waited for him inside the doorway. A letter rested on his palm. Garrett tore the seal and scanned the brief contents.

My Lord,

It will be a great pleasure to have your company at Greenly Court. Your Uncle Charles was a close friend and I will be honored to join friendship with you as well. We are home for the afternoon, if you wish to pay a call for tea.

Yours faithfully,
John Carrington

Garrett folded the letter and slipped it into his waistcoat pocket. This afternoon he would meet his fate. In no way would he let on to the gentleman that his intention was to see Miss Miriah Carrington. It would do him no good to rush his fences when he was not familiar with the young lady. If she was the one he was thinking about, she had seemed shy when he set eyes on her last at a country dance.

A thought struck him. Though the solicitor had not mentioned it, was it possible Mr. Carrington knew of the arranged marriage?

Drawing in a deep, steady breath, Garrett dismounted Danté and turned him over to the waiting groom while his gaze took in the unimposing structure. The house was much smaller than Rashley Hall or Finchston Park. Of course, Mr. Carrington was a country gentleman, not a titled man of wealth and holdings as Garrett's father and uncle had been. Pebbles grated under his boots as he stepped toward the portico of the house. There was no grand staircase or imposing entry, just four simple steps. From the Jacobean look of the house, it reminded him of a church.

The door creaked open to reveal a portly gentleman with long, bushy, white side burns, who stood half a head shorter than Garrett. He surmised the smiling man to be Mr. Carrington.

'Welcome, Lord Rashley, to our humble home.'

A small lady, whose gray hair peeked

from the edges of a lace cap, came to stand at her husband's elbow. Mrs. Carrington curtsied as her husband bowed.

'Yes, please do come in and welcome, Lord Rashley.'

Garrett noticed her face was delicately lined.

'Thank you.' He stepped inside. After his eyes adjusted to the dim light, he glanced about at the Jacobean plasterwork along the ceiling of the hall. 'You have a lovely home.'

At one end, a fine oak staircase led to the second floor, the structure being no larger than two stories and an attic. Not the least imposing, the house felt warm due to his impression that the inhabitants were of a friendly nature.

Mrs. Carrington led the way to the parlour on the left of the hall. The room was cozy and cream-colored, adding to its brightness. Garrett stood while she rang for tea then sat after she had done so.

The door opened and all heads

turned at the sight of a petite auburn-haired young lady. Bounding to his feet, he noticed her gaze barely meeting his before she looked down at her slippers.

Good heavens, she is even more shy than I remembered, he thought. Wait a moment. She is not blond.

'Lord Rashley, this is our eldest daughter, Ann,' Mr. Carrington made the introductions.

'Ann is engaged to be married three months from now to Mr. Sumner of Exeter,' Mrs. Carrington added. Garrett let out the breath he was unconsciously holding. This was not his intended bride. The other sister must be the blond. He felt a momentary reprieve.

'My felicitations, Miss Carrington.' He bowed slightly, then turned to Mr. Carrington and forgetting his intention to appear disinterested in seeing Miss Miriah, he asked, 'Do you not have another daughter? Miss Miriah Carrington, I believe?'

'Why, indeed we do. She is away from home for a time. Her uncle is a vicar and recently widowed. He needed her until he finds a suitable housekeeper.'

'I see.' A log fell in the grate and Garrett stared at sparks from the popping wood in waiting silence.

A maid bustled in with the tea tray and biscuits, setting them down on the table close to Mrs. Carrington.

Garrett accepted his tea and took a sip of the hot brew. A moment later, he smiled at Miss Carrington as she offered him a choice of teacakes. He looked across at Mr. Carrington to find the gentleman studying him over the rim of his teacup.

'Perhaps you wish to meet Miriah, Lord Rashley?'

Garrett didn't have to look at the two ladies to know that their attention was directed at him after such a statement.

'Why, yes. I met her once, but that was four years ago. I had hoped to see her again.' It didn't hurt, he supposed, to sound a little disappointed that she was not there. After all, she was his prime reason for visiting.

'But, of course.' Mr. Carrington's teacup clinked against the saucer. 'I have only to send a letter to her this afternoon.'

'Is she so far away?' Like the ticking of a clock behind him, his freedom was ebbing away as well.

'Swithingham is less than twenty miles from here. She could be home by tomorrow afternoon.'

'It is very convenient that she is close by then.' He bit into the sweet treat. After swallowing it, he tipped the cup to his lips once more.

Mr. Carrington turned the conversation to farming and livestock. His wife joined in with amusements to be had in the village, who was ailing, and news of a neighbor who had just given birth to twins. Miss Carrington sat quietly, glancing up at him on occasion. A hint of a smile touched her lips.

'I remember, Miss Carrington, that you were a very good dancer when last we met.' Garrett remarked on a guess.

'Thank you.' She blushed at his words. He hoped, for her sake, that she was better acquainted with Mr. Sumner and that the man had the talent needed to draw the young lady out of her shyness.

A fleeting thought crossed his mind. What was Miss Miriah Carrington like? If she wasn't the shy sister, why couldn't he remember her?

After tea, he took his leave. On the way home his mind raced back to the time of his last visit to Finchstonbury and the assemblies. He had danced with several young ladies. Which one was Miriah? There were two young ladies with blond hair and one was rather chatty. Surely that wasn't Miriah. He didn't have the patience for constant chatter. Now that he thought about it, there was another young lady with dark hair and pouty lips that had struck his fancy. But now that he was older, he knew she was not what he wanted in a wife.

Shrugging his shoulders, he turned the spirited Thoroughbred toward the home woods.

* * *

'Father, why was it necessary for me to rush home?' Miriah Carrington peered at her father with anticipation as he sat before the crackling fire in the library. He didn't look any more out of sorts than Mother had. 'I assumed Mother was ill and that I would find her abed this afternoon.' She kissed her father's forehead, stood back and tugged on the fingers of her gloves then slipped them off.

'Ah. I'm sorry if I alarmed you, Mya. I simply wished for your return.' He gestured with his hand for her to sit in the chair in front of his desk, then added 'We had a visit from our new neighbor.'

'And who might that be, Papa?' A light laugh escaped her. 'I don't recall anyone moving into the vicinity.'

'Remember old Mr. Brownhill? He passed on six months ago, or so.'

'Why, yes I recall. So, you mean to say Finchston Park has a new resident?' She turned round eyes on her father. 'And you wished me to return home for the express purpose of meeting this new neighbor?'

'Indeed.' He nodded, then added with merriment in his voice, 'We had a visit from Lord Rashley, just yesterday. The Rashley who lately returned from the Peninsular War.'

'Lord Rashley?' Her pulse quickened. In her dreams, day or night, her knight-errant bears the handsome likeness of Garrett Rashley.

'Yes. The nephew to the late Mr. Brownhill you know.'

'His visit signifies nothing. In all probability he has paid calls on other families in the village as well.' For a moment she stared into space and visualized looking up into his light colored eyes. His tousled medium brown curls had reminded her of pinecones from her ambling in the woods.

'I think he has not.' Mr. Carrington broke into her musings.

'And how have you come to such a conclusion, Papa? Did he hasten to our door the moment he arrived in the village?' She didn't wish to build her hopes that Lord Rashley had come to see her.

'Indeed, he did arrive day before yesterday, but he sent a missive ahead, franked from Surrey, requesting to pay his respects.'

Miriah digested this piece of information with suspicion. She recalled hearing stories of a broken engagement since she had seen him last.

Her father cleared his throat and continued. 'And what is more, he asked about you by name, before your mother or I had mentioned you.'

Her head shot up and she stared, wide-eyed at her father. 'I scarce can believe that.' She felt heat rise in her cheeks.

'Yet, it is true just the same. After meeting Ann, he looked about, then inquired if we had another daughter.'

'You see, he only mentioned my name after hearing Ann was already spoken for. It is highly preposterous that he would remember me after only two dances over four years ago. Besides I doubt he would even have reason to recollect my name.'

'There you are wrong. He did recall your name, for we had not mentioned it. And what is more, he asked as to your whereabouts and what distance you were from home. In fact, he was most pleased when I informed him you could be home as soon as this afternoon. Now what do you say to that, Mya?'

'Well, Papa,' she stammered, 'surely there is some other explanation to be had.'

'Indeed, and that is to say he has his sights set on you, my dear.'

'Papa, don't be ridiculous.' She stood and padded over to the narrow window.

Could he have paid more attention to her than she thought? Yet, he was engaged to another since then.

'Now, hurry along up to your room and freshen up. I dare say we will expect the gentleman shortly.' He pushed himself out of the rosewood chair and stepped up behind her. 'And have a little faith, my girl.'

His hands against her shoulders, her father turned her toward the door and gently urged her out of his domain.

Miriah trudged up the wooden stairs. Was Papa right in mentioning faith? Could Lord Rashley be the answer to her prayers for a husband? She smiled to herself at the thought of divine intervention and her steps became lighter as she neared her room.

She splashed water onto her face, neck, and arms, then blotted the dampness with a towel. It was comforting to be in her old room again. It was much smaller than the one at the parsonage, but it was her room. The mulberry bed cover reflected her intense passion, and the pale ivy print paper on the walls soothed her soul. Like her inner self, the room's colors were a contradiction of her feelings.

Pulling open her wardrobe, she reached for the blue sprigged muslin. Amy, the housemaid, came in to help her dress. Butterflies fluttered in the pit of Miriah's stomach as she merely thought about Lord Rashley as Amy smoothed her fair hair.

Perhaps Lord Rashley had forgotten her penchant for droning on in idle chatter, as she was wont to do when she was nineteen. This would be her chance to show him how much she had changed. Yet, she did slip up on occasion. She hoped today would not be one of those anxious times. She always chatted when she was nervous. It was possible he would turn tail and leave as other gentlemen had done, if she started rambling again.

Before she left the room, she stared into the looking glass, studying her image closely. Her looks were no different from the plain country miss he'd stood up with four years past. Loose curls framed her oval face. A blue ribbon laced through the chignon at the back of her head matched the wider ribbon at the high waist of her pale blue dress.

Could he have been thinking of her all this time, as she had been thinking of him? She didn't wish to fool herself that he had, but her heartbeat quickened just the same.

Never had she shared her girlish tendre for Lord Rashley with anyone, not even Ann. True, she was a little envious of Ann for being betrothed, but she never let on to anyone.

Yet, no man has come close to offering for her. No one wants a chatty wife. So, why has Lord Rashley come to see her?

She touched a hand to her hair and took a deep steadying breath, then reached for the door.

Her mother and Ann were already seated in the parlour. Papa sat in his favorite high-backed chair and eyed her over the top of the Morning Post.

'You are in looks, Mya, dear,' her father spoke as she came farther into the room.

The door opened again before she had a chance to reply. Glancing over her shoulder, she noticed the stern look on Francis' face as her brother marched into the room. She preferred to see him smiling as he used to do in his salad days. Of course, that was before he become a solicitor who made his own living by taking his clients' cases to the barristers.

Perhaps he was resentful of his status as a younger son. Their older brother, Stephen, showed more patience and had a friendlier demeanor. He also stood to own this house and its lands one day. What a pity Stephen wasn't here to lift her confidence.

Miriah sighed and thanked the good Lord for making her a female whose chief obligation at the age of twenty-three was to find a husband. Unlike a man who had the responsibility of running an estate. Taking up a book, she sat on the divan beside Ann, who worked on a needlepoint design for chair cushions.

The clock chimed the half-hour. At the same instant, the sound of the knocker signaled a guest. Miriah sent up a silent prayer and tried to relax her taut nerves. Even Ann sat up straighter and dwarfed her by two inches. It seemed odd that the taller of the two was the shy one. As Miriah's mother had told her once. God had given her the presence to speak her mind because of her smallness. If only she could keep her conversation to precise words without prattling on.

The parlour door opened.

'Lord Garrett Rashley,' the maid announced.

He entered the room and bowed. Miriah stole a glimpse up at him as a flood of memories came back to greet her. He was exceedingly handsome, and tall. She averted her eyes lest he thinks ill of her for staring.

Her heartbeat quickened as it had the last time she had seen him. Back then, she had the opportunity to touch his hand as he took her through the steps of a country dance. For over four years she had relived that dance in her dreams.

' . . . my youngest daughter, Miriah. Lord Rashley.'

Embarrassed for missing part of the introduction, she looked up to find the subject of her thoughts gawking at her. He looked as if he had seen a ghost.

2

'Miss Miriah Carrington.' Lord Rashley masked his expression and took her hand in his. As he bowed, his spicy scent tickled her nose. The tingly sensation of so long ago came over her again. Did he feel it, too? If he did, he was poised enough not to let it show. His eyes, the color of a clear blue sky, stared back at her. For once, she couldn't think of a thing to say.

'Please take a chair, my lord.' Her father waved him to a chair across from her. As she sat between her mother and Ann, she noticed Francis standing aloof with a somber face. If she didn't know any better she would think he was blue deviled that Lord Rashley was here instead of Francis' particular barrister friend, Mr. Hastings. She had reminded Francis time after time that she had no feelings for the older man.

Lord Rashley's soothing voice brought her back to the present. 'I trust you had a pleasant journey, Miss Miriah Carrington?'

'Why yes, my lord.' His inquiry released a flood of words from her lips. 'The weather is remarkably fresh during the spring months. And the blooms of the bluebells and golden dandelions so pleasant to behold, don't you think? Not to be outwitted by the pleasant perfumed scent of the sweet woodruff and its ivory blooms.' She drew a breath and gestured with her hands as she continued, 'The sun is so vividly bright and the skies so blue and clear. I vow I am in my element driving through the country-side in May. Of course there were those four straight days of horrid thunderstorms at the beginning of the month, but that is another matter. And how about yourself?' She ended her babbling on a nervous laugh.

His lips twitched before turning up in a half-smile.

'I enjoy spring as much as I do autumn.'

She berated herself mentally for her babbling. Why was it that she forgot how to control her vexing habit in front of the one man that meant so much to her?

'Speaking of the out-of-doors, how did you find the fields and cattle at Finchston Park? Has the steward looked after the place properly?' Mr. Carrington asked, diverting Lord Rashley's attention.

Miriah took the opportunity to collect herself and study Lord Rashley more closely. His tousled hair was almost a sandy color mingled with acorns, the same shade as the pony she had ridden at Grandpapa's when she was a child. Their conversation continued, and she sat mesmerized by Lord Rashley's deep melodic voice. It soothed her much like keys to the pianoforte while playing a slow, romantic tune.

The scar on his jawline wasn't there

when last she saw him. He must have acquired it during the war. If given the opportunity, she vowed to ask which battle he had fought.

'My lord, have you visited the parish church since your arrival?' Francis spoke for the first time, interrupting her thoughts.

'Why, no. Does it warrant my attention? Is it in need of repairs?' Lord Rashley leveled a look on Francis.

'Not to my knowledge. But it is your responsibility, or have you forgotten that fact?' Francis' accusing tone was not lost on Miriah.

'I am very well aware of my responsibilities and I shall converse with the local vicar in due time. You speak as if you expect me to withdraw all funds from the church.' The chill in Lord Rashley's voice reached his eyes as he glared across the room at Francis. If he had looked at her in such a manner, she knew she would shiver to her toes. She slanted a look at Francis.

A knife could cut the tension in the

room. Miriah glanced up at Lord Rashley's stone features to see a muscle flex at his jaw.

'I am only implying that your dear uncle took an active part as patron. He saw to the needs of the vicar and the parish. It is my concern that you carry on the role with some degree of continuity.'

'And why would I not?'

'There are those who believe you are not a religious man. Then, it is understood that you will apply your monies in other endeavors, Lord Rashley. Is that a safe assumption?'

Where did Francis come up with such a story? Miriah had never heard such talk.

'I shall honour my duty to the church. As for being religious, that is neither here nor there. I owe you no explanation on that account.'

She spoke the first thought that came to mind to divert his attention from the annoyance of Francis.

'Lord Rashley, would you care for some tea and macaroons?'

40

★ ★ ★

Garrett spurred Danté across the open meadow. A brisk run would do them both good. The sun shone bright overhead and a crisp breeze ruffled his hair beneath his beaver hat. Over the ridge and down toward the placid lake, horse and rider kept up their steady pace. Near an outcropping of oaks, he pulled up the reins and dismounted.

'Of all the girls in the county, why did it have to be the chatterbox?'

He looked over at Danté, who responded with a flick of his ears. Garrett imagined the Thoroughbred as more than a horse; Danté was his confidant.

'She makes up for her older sister's shyness excessively. And that 'holier than thou' brother. Reminding me of my responsibilities. Inquiring if I am religious. If I want Miss Miriah Carrington to know my feelings on religion, I will speak to her in private, not in front of her family. It is simply none of their business. Her brother is attempting to paint an unpleasant picture of me in Miss Miriah's eyes. But why am I not a worthy suitor?'

Squatting down on the bank, he reached for a tall piece of grass next to his knee and snapped it off an inch above the ground.

'Can you imagine what life with her will be like, Danté? Not a quiet moment to be had, for sure. What compelled Uncle Charles to saddle me with one such as her? It is absurd, indeed!' He stood abruptly and threw the remnant of grass aside.

'Of course, her sparkling blue-gray eyes gazed directly at me as I talked to her. She showed a keen interest in my every word.' He inhaled the scent of the swaying grass.

'I suppose there is nothing, but that I should court the miss. Perhaps I shall simply ignore her incessant drivel.'

Taking Danté's reins, he mounted and turned the horse toward the home woods. It wouldn't hurt to write his sister, Abigail, and ask advice. If necessary, he would invite her to Finchston Park along with his young niece and nephew. Not that he wanted company just yet, but he desperately needed to talk to one of the two women he did trust.

★ ★ ★

The next afternoon, Garrett stood on the threshold of Greenly Court. The maid showed him into the familiar cream colored parlour where Mrs. Carrington and Miss Miriah Carrington sat reading.

'Lord Rashley, ma'am.' The maid curtsied and closed the door behind her.

'I trust I am not interrupting.' He spoke as he bowed to the ladies.

'Why no, not at all, my lord.' Mrs. Carrington waved a hand in her daughter's direction and added, 'we were simply reading.'

'It is a lovely afternoon, and I came

to inquire if Miss Miriah Carrington would care to take a walk up the lane, since she is fond of spring.' His gaze moved across the bright room to find the lady in question looking at him open mouthed before she glanced down at the book resting in her lap, recollecting herself.

A rose tint flared over her fair skin. He smiled inwardly at the effect he had on her.

'What a lovely suggestion,' Mrs. Carrington said.

'Allow me to fetch my wrap. I will be but a moment, my lord.' Miss Miriah Carrington curtsied and hastened from the room.

'Is Mr. Carrington about?' He slanted a look toward Mrs. Carrington.

'No, my lord. He and Francis have gone to visit an acquaintance, but they shall return shortly.'

'I see.' Garrett found the thought of Francis' absence satisfying. He didn't relish another confrontation with the man.

Shortly, Miss Miriah Carrington returned to the parlour with a fawn-colored Norwich shawl draped about the shoulders of the brown print muslin dress.

Garrett led her down the hall, her gloved hand resting ever so lightly on his arm. The pleasant scent of lavender touched his nose as he studied her fine facial features and chignon at the back of her head. Once outside, she dropped her hand to join it with the other behind her back. He followed suit. They walked in silence for a few minutes before she spoke.

'Are you settled in at the Park, my lord?' The cool breeze sent a stray flaxen curl over one of her blue-gray eyes. With a wave of her hand she flicked it away.

'That depends on what you mean by settled. My things are unpacked and in place. However, I am trying to adjust to the status of owner as opposed to a houseguest.'

A smile grew from her shapely lips to

her twinkling iridescent eyes. He saw a gleam of interest in their depths.

'I am sure it shan't take too very long before you are comfortable with being the lord of the manor, so to speak. You certainly look the part of the master.' There was sincerity in her voice that gave him to wonder if she had ever left the countryside.

'Have you been to London?' He asked.

'No, I have not. Nor, may I add, do I wish to go to London. I have heard so many tales that I feel I would not like it.' She quickly amended, 'But that certainly does not mean it is not a nice place to visit. It is just that if I had been there I might have a different opinion of it. I don't mean to say — '

'You need not explain on my behalf. I simply wanted to ascertain if you had been.'

'Oh.' She looked away, perplexed.

'My apologies. It was not my intent to interrupt.'

'On the contrary. I should apologize for my rambling. Mother warned me against my chattering ways. I seem not to know when to hold my tongue. It is a failing I have. I am sure you have noticed it, my lord.' She ended her conversation with a little laugh. Another habit she had, he mused. He found that one strangely appealing.

'Perhaps you could teach your sister, Miss Carrington, to speak more openly like you, and she could teach you how to be less talkative like her. Then the two of you would be as perfect as two peas in a pod.' He smiled down at her.

'What an . . . odd way of putting things, to be sure.'

'Why not indulge me, and tell me what this beautiful spring day means to you.' His gaze took in the land, the trees, and the sky.

'That is easy enough for me.' They came to stand on a slope that wandered down over a green field. A herd of diminutive Red Dexter cattle grazed peacefully below. He watched her take a panoramic view of all she could see, noticing the top of her golden-blond tresses on a level with his shoulder. The expression on her face changed as he imagined her searching for the appropriate words to describe the scene before her. Then she spoke in a serious vein.

'This beautiful spring day is a gift I treasure from heaven above. There is the smell of freshness that only God can give to each of us. There is newness of life in the spring calves, and lambs, and ducklings, and baby birds. New life is everywhere. You can inhale the sweetness of the flowers.'

Her voice had an ethereal quality he hadn't noticed before, and found it pleasing. He listened intently as she continued. 'There is an honesty about the land that has nothing to do with spring in particular. It is just here in the land. I want to stay and admire the country forever. What more could one want out of life than the peace God gives one? And it is here for me.' She paused a moment, then added, 'And you?'

'You see all that?'

'Yes.' She turned to him. 'Now, what do you see, Lord Rashley?'

Looking away, he said, 'I am too cynical to see anything as clearly as you.'

'Follow me and I shall show you the way and the truth the Good Book says.'

At her Biblical recital, he stiffened. For he did not wish to hear those words.

'I am not a religious man,' he answered.

'I understand. And it is beyond me to judge you for your feelings.'

He threw her a glance to find her scrutinizing him. At that moment, he admired her for standing up to what she believed, knowing his feelings were different from hers. It struck him that she was no milk and water miss.

'Do you enjoy fishing, my lord?'

The change of subject caught him off guard. 'What?'

'I said, do you enjoy fishing?' Laughter filled her voice as she smiled up at him.

'Of course. What man doesn't?'

'Francis for one.' She answered. He flinched at the mention of her brother's name. 'He'd rather have his nose in a law book. But that is neither here nor there. Would you like to go fishing in our pond tomorrow or some other day? I love to fish myself.'

There was merriment about her that he found infectious and it glossed over any uneasiness he temporarily felt. He returned her smile.

'Ladies don't fish.'

'Well I happen to, my lord. My older brother, Stephen, taught me the intricacies of the sport. And Papa never minded when I joined him down by the water. Perhaps, it is your belief that ladies are too delicate for such sport. Then, I feel extremely sorry for your narrow mindedness. I believe in plain speaking. I hope you do not hold that against me.'

'Indeed not. I find I much prefer it. But you needn't tell me something I had suspected on my own.' After he spoke, a shadow fell over them and both looked up into the sky. He glanced down at her upturned face. The color in her eyes reflected the hue in the dark cloud. 'What is nature telling you now, Miss Miriah Carrington?'

'It says fishing is highly unlikely tomorrow, for it shall rain.' Her gaze moved from the heavens to him. Then she amended, 'It will have to be day after the morrow I am afraid.'

"The clouds in the sky told you that? I have seen clouds come and go without the benefit of rain. Why do you propose rain?'

'I have lived in the country all my life. It is second nature for me to watch the weather.'

'Perhaps we had best return to the house. For I am quite sure I have overstayed my visit.' He offered her his arm and led her down the hill and toward the house.

'Would you like a glass of lemonade and a scone before you take your leave?'

'I really ought to be going.'

'But you mustn't hurry off. Father and Francis are to return shortly. Unless of course, you do not wish to see them?'

Did she sense his reason for leaving was Francis? What a remarkably perceptive young lady Miss Miriah Carrington was, to be sure.

'I shall stay long enough to have lemonade. Then I really must be going.'

As he walked along the stone drive, she squeezed his arm lightly and spoke.

'I completely forgot. Francis and I are to leave day after the morrow. I am in charge of the parish social and have to return to tie up loose ends. It is to be Saturday on the church grounds in Swithingham. Would you wish to join us? Papa and Mama are coming for the day. There will be puppet shows, three leg races and games.'

Looking into her eyes, Garrett was drawn to the warmth he saw in them.

The desire to please her was strong. And the feeling was new to him.

'I would be happy to attend if that is your wish,' he answered, though he knew he would feel like a fish out of water at a church social.

'I most certainly would like that.' She smiled warmly up at him, then just as quickly her expression grew serious. 'You mustn't go if it is not what pleases you. I cannot bear to cause you vexation if you really do not wish to join us.'

'Believe me. It would take a grave act to force me into doing what I do not wish to do, Miss Carrington.'

★ ★ ★

Three days later, Miriah strolled past a gathering of children.

'Pray, what is he doing here?' Francis' cutting words surprised Miriah and she turned to see the subject of her thoughts riding up to the churchyard. Hadn't Lord Rashley said

53

he wished to please her? Her heart turned somersaults.

She watched Lord Rashley scanning the crowd from the back of the big Thoroughbred as he reigned it in to a stop. He dismounted with ease and straightened his beige greatcoat over his lean frame. Buckskin breeches hugged his well-formed legs to the tops of his brown, knee-length boots. He wore a wool beaver hat atop his loose brown curls. Brows shaped as birds' wings, arched above a pair of searching blue eyes. His nose was as straight as an average aristocrat. The angular shape of his jaw brought to mind his determination. To her, he was the most handsome man she had ever encountered. She inhaled and let her breath out slowly.

'Why doesn't he go back to London where he belongs?' Francis sidestepped a lad pushing a hoop.

'How unkind of you.' She noticed Lord Rashley stood a head taller above other men in the church crowd. His gaze found her and she felt the familiar butterflies flitter inside her body.

'I have seen his sort before, they haven't a care for their responsibility toward their tenants or to the church. Now, Rupert Hastings is quite different. He stays up into the night to plan his cases and final speeches to plead before the bench. He's an honest, respectable man.'

'How odd. You failed to mention Mr. Hastings' faith. Does he have faith, Francis? Is he so impeccable that you must stand behind him even if he doesn't? Yet you claim Lord Rashley to be the worst sort of fellow. It is true he has little faith . . . ' Her gaze held Lord Rashley's as he wove his way through running children toward them.

'You mean no faith! It is likely that he has never graced the pews of a church in his whole life. I have heard stories of his rakish existence. Believe me, he is beyond redemption from what I have heard.'

'Francis! God does not give up on lost sheep. Why must you?' She turned and walked through the maze of boisterous parishioners to stand in front of Lord Rashley. Her heart determined that she would see him enjoy this beautiful day.

'Lord Rashley, I am so pleased you have come.' She curtsied to his bow.

'I told you I would. Did you not believe me?' There was a teasing quality in his mellow voice.

'But of course.' She flashed him her most gracious smile. 'May I offer you some refreshment?'

'I would prefer to stretch my legs first.'

'A stroll would be most pleasing to me also.' As she walked beside him, she inhaled his woodsy scent. Then her arm brushed against his. The touch sent a spark through her body. She glanced up to find him looking the other direction as if he found the small crowd to be of interest all of a sudden. It was as if he felt uneasy with her.

A cat darted between them, followed by a barking dog. He reached a hand to steady her, then dropped it. Her arm felt warm from his touch.

'What is that group of children doing over there?' Her eyes followed the direction he pointed. Adults and other children were shouting at young boys who were attempting to run in pairs.

'Oh, they are racing with a leg tied to each other.' She laughed.

'Will they not fall?'

'It is a distinct possibility that they will. Do not tell me, sir that you have never participated in a three-legged race. 'Tis a lot of fun. Let us go and cheer them on. What do you say?'

He looked down at her with sparkling eyes and a broad smile then offered his arm to her. She found herself walking faster to keep up with his long stride. His laugh was rich and warm, and she found herself laughing as well.

'I wish I were a child right now. Then I would not be envious of what these children have, but would share it with them.'

Her heart went out to him.

'And what is it they have that you covet?' She had to ask. Was it loneliness she saw in the depths of his cool blue eyes? If so, she wanted nothing more than to erase the look with one of warmth and love.

'This is a social is it not?' he asked, a bitter edge of cynicism in his voice. 'Let us go about and enjoy it.'

Children from the three-legged race giggled nearby.

He glanced over her shoulder and she turned around. A makeshift stage stood below a stand of chestnut trees and children and adults sat on the grass watching a puppet play. She fell in step with him as he changed directions and strolled toward the audience lounging in the shade.

At the back of the small crowd, Miriah sat and pulled her skirt under her legs. He dropped down beside her and rested his arms across his knees. The lines of his face softened as he watched and laughed along with the others. Since his arrival at the social, she saw in him a sensitive man hiding behind indifference. She knew that, deep inside he was hurting, and one day she would learn the truth of his pain.

'Miss Miriah Carrington.' Miriah turned at the lilting voice behind her. It was Rebecca Sneed who exuded beauty from her round hazel eyes and pouty lips set in porcelain skin, framed with a thick mane of black hair. 'You have done a great job for your uncle in organizing this nice social,' Miss Sneed said as she lowered herself beside Miriah and glanced pointedly across Miriah's lap. 'Lord Rashley, I never thought to see you here.'

Miriah looked back at Lord Rashley to see him staring at Miss Sneed. He blinked his eyes a couple of times and looked dumbfounded.

'Yes, well . . . you see I am here. And I'm sorry I do not recall your name.' He seemed to tell the truth but Miriah doubted that any man could forget this lovely young woman's name. Now that she thought of it, she was more surprised that he remembered her own name. Miriah had no claim to prettiness or great fortune. Although she does have connections on her mother's side.

Swallowing her pride, she introduced the charmer to Lord Rashley.

'May I present Miss Rebecca Sneed?'

'Oh, yes, Miss Sneed. I do believe we danced in Finchstonbury when last I was at my uncle's, before I left for the war.'

'Of course, my lord. And a very fine dancer you are, I recall. Perhaps we can share a few more dances at the next assembly in Finchstonbury or here about.'

Miss Sneed's high-pitched laughter grated on Miriah's nerves like a squeaking door. She wished the lady would find a diversion and leave her and Lord Rashley in peace. She immediately chastised herself for her unchristian-like attitude toward the lady. But she could not change her desire to be alone with Lord Rashley.

'Are you staying at Finchston Park, my lord?'

'Yes. I have recently moved in. My uncle has departed, you see — '

'Yes, yes, I remember that,' Miss Sneed broke in. 'But I was not aware that you had actually moved into the estate. Surely you are in want of a lady to put it to rights for you, sir.'

Miriah looked away and sent up a silent prayer to hold her tongue. It would not do to loose her temper at the impertinent Miss Sneed. A sharp comment wouldn't recommend her to Lord Rashley either. And she did want to please him.

'You think I cannot manage my own estate, house and all? I assure you that I am not a simpleton.'

Miriah breathed a sigh of relief. It appeared he was of the same feeling as she about Miss Sneed's forward nature.

'You take my meaning wrong, sir. I assure you. I simply meant . . . '

'I know what you meant, Miss Sneed. But I prefer to handle matters my own way. I always have and always will. And a lady will never run my life for me. For I prefer to handle my affairs myself. Do you understand my meaning?'

'Yes, of course, to be sure.' The lady looked chagrined before she glanced over at the church. 'Excuse me, Miss Miriah Carrington, Lord Rashley. I believe my father is looking for me.'

Lord Rashley helped Miss Sneed to her feet. Miriah made to stand, but was stayed by his hand and a look. The beauty walked away, and Lord Rashley sat back down on the grassy slope, close to Miriah.

'What a brazen young lady.' His breath warmed her neck as he whispered close to her ear. 'If I were her father, I would lock her in a room until she learned her manners.'

Miriah turned to find herself inches from his handsome face. His gaze held hers as he uttered, 'I expected to hear a diatribe of plain speaking come from your lips.'

'I came very close to voicing my opinion, then I thought better of it.' Her gaze went to his lips. His smile grew to show his straight white teeth. Blinking, she looked up as warmth stole over her cheeks.

'Miriah, you are not overseeing the food tables for Uncle Henry.' She jerked her head a degree to where Francis stood behind them. His irritated tone brought her back to reality. 'Besides, Mr. Hastings would be offended if he were here to see you sitting so close to my sister, Lord Rashley. Please remember where you are and remove yourself, sir.'

'What?' Lord Rashley leaped to his feet.

'Francis!' Miriah jumped up without assistance as she and Lord Rashley spoke at the same time.

'I did not know Miss Miriah Carrington had an understanding with another.' Lord Rashley's sharp glare directed at Francis could have cut ice on a frozen pond. A muscle in his jaw tightened.

'But I do not have an understanding with Mr. Hastings or anyone else for that matter.' Lord Rashley slanted her a look. 'Francis is merely speaking from wishful thinking on his part.' Miriah followed Lord Rashley's gaze to her hand clinching his sleeve. With the speed of lightening she released her hold on him. 'Francis does not speak for me, my lord.'

'Miriah — ' Francis tried to cut into the conversation.

'I was in hopes that he did not.' Lord Rashley's eyes searched hers with what she thought was understanding in them.

'Lower your voice, Miriah. People are beginning to look.' She glanced back at Francis who peered about him. Red heat covered his face.

'You should have thought about that before you confronted me. And besides, I am here to help my uncle. He commended me on how well I organized the tables not more than three-quarters of an hour ago. All that matters is that he is pleased. Furthermore, it is no concern of yours, or Mr. Hastings as far as that goes, whom I choose to socialize with at this or any other function I may attend in future.'

She marched away, leaving two sets of eyes to stare after her.

Francis knew she had a temper, and he shouldn't push her as he had done. For her sake, it would have been better that Lord Rashley didn't know of her temper. More than likely, he saw her in a less favorable light, now.

Approaching the food table, she looked about. Nothing appeared amiss to her. There were plenty of meats, cheeses, breads, and desserts.

She balled her hands at her sides. This was Francis' way of coming between her and his lordship. It appeared to her that Francis was playing the matchmaker and attempted to push her in the direction of his associate, Mr. Hastings. She seethed with anger toward her brother, for the single state was preferable to being wed to a man close to her father's age. Even if Mr. Hastings was good looking in an older gentlemanly way. A chill stole over her and she shivered.

Heavy steps came up beside her.

'Let us go for a walk, shall we?' Lord Rashley's mellow voice was uncompromising yet oddly gentle. 'Please.'

Her shoulders drooped and she turned to walk beside him toward a copse of trees. Stopping under the shade of a big oak, he glanced back in the direction of the church then looked down at her.

'You gave your brother a set down he deserved. But you most likely need time to cool your heels before some unsuspecting soul speaks and you let loose that tongue of yours.' She looked down at her feet and felt ashamed of her actions. He reached his finger under her chin and raised her face to his. 'It is all right. Francis had it coming. You simply need time to compose yourself.'

She felt her lower lip tremble. He touched the pad of his thumb lightly to one corner of her mouth. 'Where is that pretty smile that warms a cloudy day?'

Her lips obeyed his touch. And he, too, smiled in return.

'Do you like to go riding? I have a sporty carriage I will allow you to drive some day. Did your older brother teach you how to handle the ribbons?'

She knew he was trying to draw her out of her somber mood.

'No, I did not have the opportunity, my lord. Would you teach me?' She laughed.

3

Sunlight sent a ray of light over the top of the low hanging clouds. The late afternoon air was warm against Garrett's face. Pulling on the reins, he slowed Danté to a walk to cool the animal and give himself opportunity to think.

Time spent alone was precious to his well-being. He had his fill of new acquaintances, and superfluous conversation hours ago at the church social. Life was changing fast enough, and he needed time to consider his future with one high-strung female.

He had felt a kinship with Miriah the instant she jumped to her feet and issued Francis a cutting set-down this afternoon. If the uncivil man were his brother, he would do the same and more.

Garrett inhaled the fresh scent of

Meadow Fox-Tail grass, mingled with the smell of a sweating horse. Birds interrupted his solitude as they chirped in the low hanging branches of trees that lined the road.

'She possesses a fighting spirit, and stands up for what she believes. I admire her for that.' He was talking more to himself than to Danté. The horse's ears perked up as if he were listening. 'I could teach her how to control that temper. If she would permit it.'

His thoughts turned to her other characteristics. There was nothing in her personality to remind him of his unfaithful mother. No, Miriah was strong-willed and spoke her mind. Sneaking off in the dark of night would not be her way. She would be forthright about her feelings and expect the same from him.

Miss Sneed, on the other hand, he did not trust at all.

'Danté.' He patted the animal's neck. 'Did you see that Sneed female? She all but threw herself at me in front of Miss Miriah. I cannot believe the audacity of that chit. She may be pretty, but she is also trouble. I must contrive never to be alone with her.'

After a momentary silence, he added, 'On the other hand, what did you think of Miss Miriah?' He waited as if he expected the horse to answer. 'Her looks are quite pleasing. With regard to her habit of rambling, she seems to be trying in earnest to change. If she fails, I will endeavor to travel to London, or go hunting with my friends on occasion.'

It was dark by the time he reined Danté in at the front of the manor. After going up to his room and quickly changing his clothes, he returned below stairs to the dining room for a quiet dinner alone.

Two servants shuffled back and forth as they carried the dishes in and out of the room. The distinct scent of poached salmon reached Garrett before the servant placed the dish in front of him. With deliberate slowness, he indulged

70

in each coarse. The meal was excellent, even if it was only for himself.

His thoughts turned to Uncle Charles, who left him an allowance to live on until he fulfilled the terms of the will. Garrett hoped he could live up to his late uncle's wishes. As much as he was against marriage, he would do anything for his uncle. And yet, there was an inkling of doubt about marriage that haunted him from his past.

As he ate, the day's events played in his head.

'Perhaps I should not have gone to the social after all.' He mumbled to himself as he placed the fork beside his plate.

'Why must I marry?' He looked up at the ceiling. 'I value my privacy. You knew that, Uncle Charles.'

He ran a hand through his hair and clasped his hands behind his head. A fleeting thought came to him from the darker side of his mind. If he married Miss Miriah Carrington, he would be rich beyond his means. Money could

71

buy him anything and take him anywhere. She was merely a resource toward that goal. The will required he marry. It didn't stipulate that they live together. Perhaps he could stay with her long enough to produce an heir, but afterward he could go where he pleased without her.

Closing his eyes, another thought flashed through his mind. His mother had taken herself off for her own pleasure. His eyes flicked open. What he was considering was not the same, was it? He still chastised his mother for the action she had taken so many years ago. And think of the pain she had caused. No, he could not do that to Miriah. What was more he could not do that to his child, unlike his mother, he could not live with the guilt his leaving would cause.

He reached for his glass of claret and swirled the dark purplish red liquid. There was nothing for it but that he should court Miriah. Yet, he preferred not to court her at her uncle's. She didn't need a distraction from finding a suitable housekeeper for her uncle. There was no telling how long that would take. In the meantime, he would patiently wait for her to return home before he began the courtship. And it wouldn't hurt to pay his half brother's family a visit.

After dinner, he marched up the stairs with resolution in each step. He resolved not to rush his fences again. After all, he had little time to himself as it was.

'Denby, pack our things. We are going to depart at first light and pay a call on Joseph in Guildford.'

'Yes, sir.' His valet headed for the dressing room and followed Garrett's directive.

A short time later, Garrett laid his head back against his thick pillow and stared into the darkness of his room. Riding over to Guildford would put distance and time between him and the goal to enhance his financial independence. What little freedom he had was his to control for the time being. He needed to take coming events much slower.

Miriah was not indifferent to him, or she wouldn't have stood up against her brother for him. Not that he wasn't capable of handling Francis. Yet, when Garrett had seen fire in her eyes, it had behooved him to see how she would handle her brother's intrusion. Garrett was not disappointed. And he admired her independence.

He remembered their earlier conversation after her father's summons when Garrett took her for a walk. The more he talked with her, the more he noticed her as quite the opposite of his mother and former fiancée. If he didn't know any better that day at the pond at her father's, he would think she was trying to pull things out of him he did not know existed. She brought up religion and caused him pain. Yet, with her keen sense of perception, she changed to the subject of fishing in a most delightful way to make him smile. What a puzzle she was, to be sure.

Never before had he known a lady who cared what he felt, other than his sister, Abigail, and Joseph's wife, Jennifer. Perhaps, Miriah did not want to be under any man's thumb.

★ ★ ★

The sky opened and a deluge of rain pounded the earth as Garrett watched from the narrow window. It hadn't been much over two weeks since he sat in this very room at Rashley Hall and learned of his fate.

'Was the spring planting done? Have you harvested the corn, Gar?' Joseph interrupted his thoughts.

'Why yes, it has been planted. But I think it needs more than two weeks to grow.' Sitting in a high-backed wing chair, Garrett stretched his legs and stared at the yellow flames. He watched the gray smoke rise up the chimney. 'The tenants have done well.'

'Has the house gone to wrack and

ruin?' Joseph leaned his head back against a cushioned chair in the library.

'The place is not in such bad repair as I had first thought. The steward has continued the upkeep after Uncle Charles' passing. I will need to refurbish the inside of the place, but I will wait until I marry and let the lady handle household duties and what have you. I understand ladies like that sort of thing. Besides, it will keep her occupied.' His tone was matter of fact.

'And what about the lady? Have you reacquainted yourself with Miss Miriah Carrington?' Joseph looked over at him with a keen eye. 'Was she the sister you envisioned her to be?'

'Not really. But — ' Garrett smiled at his older brother before adding, 'she is pleasing to the eye. Yet she does tend to rattle on at times.'

'But can you overlook such a flaw in her?'

'At first I did not think so, but then her manner of speaking improved upon me. I think she is making a conscious effort to quell her chatty way.' He gazed unseeing into the fire in the grate, and continued. 'She may inquire after your past, yet she knows when she has touched on a sensitive subject. Then with a spark of humor she turns the conversation around and makes you laugh. It is quite refreshing, really. I feel that she does not so much want to be entertained as she desires to entertain.'

'She sounds a veritable paragon.'

'Not a paragon exactly. She is a person of deep faith though. And she sees things through the eyes of that faith.'

'That is not a bad quality to have in a wife.' Joseph spoke softly. 'In fact, it is the very quality you need in a wife. She may teach you a thing or two about the necessity of faith.'

'You know my feelings on that subject. Don't play the father with me on that issue.' Garrett sat up to rest his arms over his knees to get closer to the fire.

'What about her looks? Is she flaxen,

raven, redhead, or brunette? I have forgotten what you said at the reading of the will.' Joseph moved to a chair opposite his.

'My mother's hair.' He whispered.

'Blond hair does not make her the same person as your mother. It is what is inside the person, not the color of the hair or eyes that make a person act as another. When will you learn that fact, Gar?'

'When I looked at her that first time, Joseph, I saw my mother's flaxen hair. Then too, Miss Miriah Carrington's features are petite like Dorothea's.' Garrett put his hands to his head and ran his fingers through his curls. 'I was duped once — could it possibly happen again?' He groaned and bowed his head.

He felt Joseph's hand on his back as his half brother came to stand beside him and massaged the tautness of his muscles at the base of his neck.

'All I can say is that your uncle must have had his reasons why the two of you should be together. It is highly unlikely that he would have chosen the first female that came to mind.' After a few moments of silence, Joseph spoke again. 'Mayhap, this marriage plan of your Uncle Charles' was meant to be a new beginning for you.'

Garrett raised his head and turned sideways to speak. 'She spoke of new beginnings.'

'Who?'

'Miss Miriah Carrington. She was describing the outdoors, and what it meant to her at this time of year. I recall her mentioning new beginnings.'

'I think you had better hurry back to Finchston Park and marry this girl. She sounds too good to lose to another.'

'But she has this brother, a solicitor, who appears not to like me, and the feeling is mutual. He has another man in mind for her to marry. She did ring a peel over him about it. Said she did not have an understanding with this other fellow or anyone else. Hastings I believe is the man's name. And she said

Francis does not speak for her.'

'Ah, she speaks her own mind.' Joseph turned his back to the fire.

'Indeed, she does.'

'Is this other fellow, Hastings, close by?'

'Evidently not, or he would have put in an appearance at the church social.'

Garrett shared with Joseph details of where Miriah had been and of her father sending notice for her to return home. He told of his attendance at the church social. He omitted the part about seeing Rebecca Sneed.

'So you see, I did not want to appear overly enthusiastic. Everything was progressing far too quickly as it was.'

'Cold feet, hey?'

'No. I needed time to think. And what can be done about her brother? How can I keep from causing pain in the family when he is likely to cause a stir over my request for her hand in marriage?'

'Let us put our heads together, shall we?' Joseph walked to the window.

Garrett stood up and began to pace the room. 'Is her brother protective over her? Maybe he is looking out for her security, do you suppose? Or is he only interested in her for his own selfish reasons?'

'He is not looking out for her welfare, that I can assure you.' Garrett put his fist to his lips and thought. 'Perhaps, if members of my family were to meet the Carrington's, they might see that as a gesture of good will and accept my suit more readily, no matter what her brother may say to the contrary.'

'It is worth a try. And it certainly will not hurt to show our support for you. When would you wish us to pay a visit?'

'Before the end of the week? Do you suppose Jennifer and the boys could be ready to leave Guildford with you by then?'

'I will discuss it with her when she returns from her afternoon calls. That is if this rain does not delay her.'

* * *

Miriah ran her hands up and down her arms as she stared out at the early summer turbulence. Rain pelted the window. Treetops were tossed about in a fitful and gusty wind. A clap of thunder roared close to the house shaking the glass in it's casing and she jumped back from the window a couple of steps.

The last conversation with Lord Rashley, when she lost her temper with Francis, played over in her mind as she continued her surveillance of the storm. Did something she said offend him and cause him to stay away? Perhaps it was because of Francis'insinuation that Garrett was sitting too close to her. Somehow she doubted that was the case. He wouldn't be moved by Francis' opinion.

Five days had passed since the church social. In that time, she had found her uncle a suitable housekeeper through a church member. After two days, Miriah had returned home.

She was disheartened to learn Lord Rashley had not called or sent notice of any kind. It was as if the earth had opened and swallowed him whole. He was nowhere to be seen. There was talk among the servants that he had simply ridden out of the county.

Was he coming back? She was not so certain.

'Mya, dear, are you taking a chill?' Her mother's voice called from her chair near the fire.

'No, Mama.' She looked back at her mother and halfheartedly smiled.

'Perhaps what you need, is a cup of chamomile tea. I'll ring Maybury.' Mrs. Carrington started to rise.

Miriah stayed her mother with words of assurance. 'Really, Mama, I am fine. I will ring for tea, but I prefer the Bohea, not the chamomile.'

'Whatever you say, dear.' Her mother sat back and eyed her curiously. 'Perhaps you are pining for a certain gentleman. Believe me when I say he will return.'

'That is absurd, I am not pining for anyone. Least of all a gentleman.' She chastised herself for the lie.

Her mother simply smiled after a long, studied look, then added, 'He has, more than not, had business to attend to elsewhere. Mark my word, you shall find him at our door soon after he returns.'

'Mama.' Miriah sighed and rolled her eyes. If only she could feel so positive. Perhaps, Francis' words had reminded Lord Rashley that he was showing her too much attention and that was not his intent after all.

She wished the rain would stop so she could go outdoors for a walk over the wet grass and smell the freshness that accompanied rain. Activity was what she needed to turn her thoughts from such folderol.

Four years ago, she had become infatuated when she first set eyes on Lord Rashley. Passage of time did nothing to dim the warmth that burned in her heart at the sight of him. Could

84

this be true love? Surely infatuation would not have lasted over the years.

Sitting in a chair closer to the heat, she stared into the yellow flame. The image of his handsome face so near to hers at the church social lit a blaze in her heart. They sat so very close, and she was mesmerized by his lips. It was obvious that he knew her thoughts at that particular moment. She had wanted him to kiss her. Would he have done so if Francis had not walked up on them? A heat, not from the hearth, burned in her cheeks.

The clank of a silver utensil against china and the scent of strong, black Bohea tea brought her out of her reverie.

★ ★ ★

Hours later, Miriah smoothed the front of her drab brown spencer then stepped outside. She drew in a deep breath. The fresh smell of rain-covered earth filled her senses with peace. An emotion she was far from feeling when thoughts of a certain gentleman haunted her. With no direction in mind, she started for a grove of trees west of the house.

Drops of water fell from nature's green canopy. She looked up to see bright sunlight flicker through the branches. Like always, the sun was brightest after a long rain. With quick steps she made it to the crest of the rise and looked back to see nothing but the path between the trees. She was alone, which suited her needs at the moment.

Walking out into the sun, she came to one of the large outcroppings of rock that dotted the landscape. The boulder was tall enough to lean her back against it. She scanned the horizon. On yonder hills, similar rock formations protruded from the green earth. They had been there for centuries. Just as suddenly, a new thought came to mind. Perhaps God wanted her to see that not everything in life is smooth as a carpet of grass. Life had its outcroppings too.

There were outcroppings between

Lord Rashley and herself even now.

Pushing away from the rock, she strolled down the hill and along a different path. It felt good just to walk and listen to the leaves rustle overhead in the trees and to feel an occasional spray of water sprinkle her head. Stopping, she looked up to see a squirrel chase another from one tree to the next. When she looked back up the path, she froze.

So intent was she on the small animals, she didn't hear the approach of the horse and rider. Astride a chestnut Thoroughbred sat the object of her thoughts. His hands rested across the pommel of the saddle, his gaze fixed on her. The horse strutted slowly toward her then stopped a few feet away.

'Miss Miriah Carrington.' Lord Rashley touched the brim of the beaver hat perched at an angle on his head, and nodded. 'I was just on my way to pay a call at Greenly. Were you heading somewhere in particular?'

'Why . . . no my lord. I was only out for a walk.'

'Would you like some company?'

'Of course. If . . . if you would like to join me.' Her heart fluttered wildly against her ribs. She couldn't believe her eyes. He was here, looming before her in buckskin breeches and a long, tan riding coat. His light-blue eyes softened as he smiled down at her.

After a moment, he climbed down and waited for her.

'Were you just beginning your walk?' He asked. 'I did not think to ask if you wished to be alone. Do you?'

'It is not imperative. And yes, I haven't gone far. I simply had to relieve the boredom of days spent indoors. It is awfully confining. Do you not agree?' She asked but didn't give him time to reply. 'I would think that you would like to be out and about as opposed to being cooped up indoors. Most men prefer to be riding daily and hunting. Or any number of things that take them out of doors. Looking over their estates, curricle rides — '

'Enough.' He interrupted her with a deep, throaty laugh. 'You have exhausted me from all the pursuits you have put me through in the last minute.'

'I am sorry. I seem to be — '

'It is quite all right.' He started to walk along the path and she fell into step with him.

She wanted to ask where he had been all week, but she didn't want to disturb the quiet that settled between them. Besides, she couldn't allow herself to show an interest in him lest he form the wrong opinion of her. It was really rather pleasant just to be near him and listen to the twigs crack below their feet.

After a few minutes, Miriah could not contain herself. 'My lord — '

Lord Rashley grabbed her arm and turned her quickly to face him as his mouth descended on hers. She didn't have time to react. No longer did she wonder what it felt like to be kissed, especially by him. His lips were warm against hers. Then the kiss ended. He stared at her for a moment, dropped the Thoroughbred's reins and put an arm about her waist and drew her to him. 'Francis is not about, is he?'

'No,' she whispered as he lowered his mouth to hers in a slow, deliberate motion. Her hands came up to rest on his shoulders. His tender lips on hers felt foreign and wonderful at the same time. Utter elation ignited within her.

Finally, he held her at arm's length and smiled down at her.

'I do believe I had better return you to the house. I fear it would be dangerous indeed, if we were to remain alone much longer.' Dropping his arms from hers, he turned and took Danté's reins in both his hands and looked back at her. 'I should not have taken advantage of you while you walked alone on your father's property. It was an ungentlemanly thing to do. However, I cannot say I am sorry I did it.'

She couldn't control the warmth that

stole into her cheeks and looked down at the ground to hide her flushed face. Not one retort could she offer him in a set down or otherwise. His kiss had indeed rendered her speechless.

'Would you rather that I leave you to your privacy and ride on ahead to the house?'

'No.' Her voice sounded high to her own ear. She stepped beside him and led the way back down the hill in silence. Never before had she been in company without uttering one word for so long. Perhaps if she spoke once more, he would be inclined to kiss her again. Yet, she didn't want him to form the wrong impression of her. For she certainly held a regard for him and his kiss only deepened that regard.

A servant took hold of his horse as Miriah led Lord Rashley to the entrance of the house. She handed her bonnet to a maid and continued to the front parlour. His steps echoed close behind her.

'Mama. Papa.' Could her parents tell

by looking at her that she had been kissed? Warmth stole over her cheeks at the thought. 'Lord Rashley came upon me as I was out for a walk and has come to call.' She stepped farther into the room and turned back to see Lord Rashley bow to both her parents.

'I presume you are as happy as I to see the sun after the past two days of rain.' He offered congenially.

'Of course. The sun brings out the best in all of us.' Mr. Carrington drawled as he motioned Lord Rashley to a chair.

'Refreshments are in order after your ride over here.' Miriah's mother smiled warmly up at the guest.

'Tea will do nicely, thank you.' He smiled at Mrs. Carrington as he sat near Miriah on the divan. 'Actually I came to offer you an invitation. My family will be arriving at Finchston Hall tomorrow. I would like all of you to come for dinner day after the morrow and meet them.'

Miriah didn't miss the speaking

glances exchanged between her parents.

'But of course, we will be happy to attend.' Mr. Carrington glanced at Miriah as he replied.

She listened intently as her father discussed government affairs with Lord Rashley. Not that she had an interest in it. But it did afford her the opportunity to study him closely, much as she had done the first time he came to call.

Her gaze took in the strong lines of his tanned features. It was an attractive face she could never tire of looking upon. Long lashes framed his almond-shaped, heaven colored eyes. The scar on his chin caught her attention as it had earlier. She reflected on how it came to be there. Perhaps a Frenchy's bayonet grazed him.

'Miriah dear, please serve the tea.' Her mother broke into her thoughts. She hadn't noticed when the servant had delivered the tray.

'Of course, Mama.' She felt her cheeks redden and hoped no one else observed her embarrassment. Stepping over to the tea tray, she poured the steeping brew.

After serving Lord Rashley and her parents, she resumed her seat and joined the conversation regarding the weather.

'I so adore the out-of-doors after a prolonged rain. It smells so fresh and alive. The colors are muted at first from the rain, but the sun glistens on the grass and leaves and makes them veritably brilliant. Do you not think so, Lord Rashley?' Miriah glanced sideways to see her mother glaring at her. As if she needed reminding that she was falling back into her old habit. She glanced over at her guest and waited for his answer.

'Yes, the colors are brilliant after the rain.' Lord Rashley took another sip of tea.

'Father, this will help your crops no doubt. There will be more grain to harvest in the fall. I am sure of it.'

'Yes, my child. Would you please pass Lord Rashley the plate of pastries,

Miriah?' Her father looked at her pointedly, reminding her that she had forgotten to offer the sweets along with the tea.

'Oh, yes. Where have my manners gone?' A light laugh escaped her as she picked up the plate of treats. 'Try the scones, they are cook's specialty.'

'Only if you will have one.' A broad grin brightened his features.

'Of course I shall. But you go first.' She waited until he picked up the sweet white breaded treat. After choosing one for herself, she returned to the sofa. It was really disconcerting for him to watch her eat. Self consciously, she dabbed a napkin to her lips to wipe away any crumbs.

'Do you expect a sizeable harvest?' Mr. Carrington asked their guest.

Lord Rashley turned his attention away from her. 'Yes, it looks very promising. The steward is well worth his keep.'

'I am glad to hear that.' Her father responded.

'Lord Rashley, you have invited us to meet your family and we know nothing about them.' Miriah spoke in the lull in the conversation. 'Please tell us, do you have brothers or sisters, or perhaps both?' Miriah had never heard him mention his family until the invitation today. It would be better to know a little about them before actually meeting them.

'Well, there is my half brother, Baron Joseph Rashley and his wife, Lady Jennifer and their three sons. Then there is my half sister, Lady Abigail and her husband, Lord Samuel Moreland and their daughter and son.'

'How nice. Are you the youngest then?' Miriah tried to guess.

'Indeed, I am. Abigail is four years my senior and Joseph is five.' He looked at her for a long moment as her father introduced another question concerning farming.

From a sideways glance, she noticed her mother rolling her eyes at her and knew she was in for a scold. But she could hardly sit still, she felt all bubbly inside. She was about to pay a visit to Finchston Hall to meet his family.

Mother had told her not to pry. Yet, he was kind enough to answer each question she threw at him even though he did not expound on any one topic.

After tea, Lord Rashley excused himself and said his good-byes.

'Until day after the morrow then, Miss Miriah Carrington.' He bowed but didn't take her hand. His gaze held hers a moment longer and she imagined a deeper emotion in them. She hoped it was so. Why else would he invite them to meet his family if he didn't have feelings for her? Her eyes followed his tall frame until the door clicked behind him.

'You see, Miriah. I told you he would come.' Her mother came up beside her and added with a worried expression. 'Why did you not pay heed to me when I tried to catch your eye. You rattled on so.'

'I am sorry, Mama. You know how I

get when I am excited.'

'Yes, dearest. I know.' Her mother patted her hand. 'Just think, we are to dine with his family.'

Miriah felt almost giddy. She floated up the stairs later to prepare for dinner with her family. In a mere two days she would be sitting to dinner in his house. How wonderful. How exciting.

4

'Joseph. There are times when she chats on aimlessly.' Sunlight filtered through the east window of his library, only to shatter as Garrett paced through the dusty beam. Perhaps the eminent end of his freedom gave him leave to be judgmental toward her. 'And yet, I did catch her frowning after one of her discourses. She was not aware that I had seen her.'

'Didn't you say that she was trying to mend her rambling way?' Joseph slunk down in a worn cloth chair and frowned. 'Quite possibly, you could offer your assistance in a round-about way.'

The remembrance of a particular kiss came to mind. Garrett turned away from Joseph. In no way could he admit he knew a surefire way to stop her idle talk. A gentleman did not betray a defenseless lady, even to a half brother, to make light of the situation.

She didn't push away from him when he kissed her. Which proved that he could gain affection, warmth and closeness.

'Do you suppose my uncle made the terms of the will known to the Carrington's before he died, Joseph?'

'The solicitor didn't let on that they knew about it. Why do you ask?'

'I have noticed that Miss Miriah Carrington is exceedingly friendly.'

'And you are suspicious because she shows an interest in you?'

'Yes. It is quite obvious she thinks I have already come into the blunt. Why else would she stand up to her brother so adamantly.' His hands clinched into fists at his sides, he added vehemently, 'His friend, Hastings, must not be worth near as much.'

'Come now. It is possible she is sincere in her feelings toward you. You said yourself that she is a lady of faith and insight. Perchance, she genuinely likes you as the person you are, not what you possess.'

Garrett tilted his head and eyed Joseph skeptically. 'I have good reason to distrust a female's motives. Do you not agree?'

Joseph shoulders slumped. 'Do you recall if she was indifferent to you before you left for the Peninsula?'

'She was naive and silly along with the other young ladies of her set. All any of them did was giggle when a gentleman showed them attention.' Crossing his arms over his chest, Garrett turned to stare out of the tall window. A brisk breeze drifted through the towering sycamores and the movement of the dull, dark green foliage mesmerized him. Another picture came to mind. That of Miriah's loose curl before she reached a fingertip up to whisk it out of her face. At the time, he thought she looked the epitome of innocence. Now he feared she might be calculating and impertinent.

Deep down he wanted to believe in

her. If only he could trust her. Fear of the past kept him from doing so.

★ ★ ★

Miriah held her hands tight in her lap as the carriage bounced along and concentrated on calming her nerves while in the presence of Lord Rashley and his family. Tonight she vowed to control the urge to hide insecurity in company with chatter. In the past four years, she had shown vast improvement. However, when he had reappeared, her old habit came back to haunt her.

'Oh my.' Her mother exclaimed as the carriage crested the hill.

Miriah and Ann turned in unison in the direction of Mrs. Carrington's gaze.

'It is an imposing structure, is it not?' Miriah's voice sounded breathless to her own ears. 'Papa, it does take your breath away at first sight.'

'Indeed, it does.' Ann echoed her sentiments.

Mr. Carrington peered out the window. 'I told you it was the grandest house in the county. With its Roman statues along the walls, the great hall is like no other. It is a shame he didn't see fit to entertain the neighbors with a ball so you ladies could have seen the place before now.' Her father spoke from the experience of past visits to his old friend, Mr. Brownhill.

Miriah viewed Finchston Park with the admiration of a child visiting the sea for the first time. A shallow dome appeared to have floated up through the roof. The set of twin stairs, leading in opposite directions from the massive front door to the ground level, reminded her of crab-pincers coming out of the rounded shell above the second floor.

Two large marble centurions stood guard from recesses between columns on either side of the front entry. Four more statues rested high above the columns and below the rotund roof. The late Mr. Brownhill must have loved

Roman architecture. She wondered if Lord Rashley was as taken with the building as his uncle? Perhaps she could make appropriate conversation with him by asking his opinions on the house.

'Have you meet Lord Rashley's half brother or half sister before, Papa?' Her stomach tightened into a knot the closer the carriage rolled toward the grandiose establishment.

'No. I have never met them.' He glanced across at her and smiled. 'I remember Charles implying that they were well-behaved children who grew up without their mother or step-mother. But I understand that the three of them are very close. In fact, Charles said that the older sister, Abigail, practically doted on young Rashley after his mother had departed.'

Miriah flashed a smile at Ann before turning to her father. 'What did his mother die from?'

'I don't think that she passed away as much as she moved on.' Mr. Carrington made to scratch his head and glanced out the window near him in a gesture that told Miriah that he did not wish to elaborate on the subject.

She glanced back at Ann who merely shrugged her shoulders and rolled her eyes. How odd, to be sure.

'Miriah, dearest. Be mindful of coming to the point of what you want to say without rambling.' Her mother's gaze brightened as she took in Miriah's features. 'Amy arranged your hair in a becoming fashion. The green silk ribbon through the curls is very stylish.'

'Thank you, Mama.' Her mother must be as nervous as she about the meeting. With Ann betrothed, Mama was focusing her attention on Miriah in finding a suitable match. She vowed to make her mother proud of her. 'I shall concentrate on being seen and not heard.'

'You needn't be so quiet, dearest, speaking to the point will be sufficient,' her mother instructed her.

The carriage rolled to a stop. A

liveried footman opened the door and lowered the step. Miriah studied the ornate balustrade, then joined her parents and Ann on the graveled drive. As she climbed the marble steps slowly behind her mother and father, she leaned her head back to view the two Roman statues of gray marble that looked out over the front lawn from their vantage point at the top of stairs.

A stone-faced butler ushered them inside a round saloon and through to a Roman Hall with no less than nine pairs of columns. Relief paintings covered the walls above more statues situated in insets between the columns. Twin fireplaces faced each other from either of the long sides of the room.

'It is overpowering, is it not?' A low, deep voice echoed across the expanse of the hall from a rear doorway.

Lord Rashley cut a dashing figure as he strolled toward them and bowed. Miriah's gaze went from the top of his shiny brown hair worn short and disheveled, to an elegant Clarence blue double breasted coat and matching pantaloon. His white silk stockings were a contrast from his dark ensemble and black kid dress pumps.

When she raised her chin, their gazes locked for the space of a second before he turned to greet her father. A reserved coolness in his eyes replaced the warmth she remembered seeing in them on his last visit. Perhaps the formal attire contributed to his distant expression. Or was he experiencing regrets that he invited her family to meet his? The stolen kiss came to mind. Was he testing her character? If so, she failed when she didn't object by pushing him away. Oh, dear. A chill tickled her spine and she ran a gloved hand down her left arm.

'I have been here on several occasions and I am always astonished by this hall, my lord.' Mr. Carrington accepted Lord Rashley's extended hand.

Miriah mentally shook off the sense of unease. Instead she focused on her father's words.

'The structure is in the style of Robert Adams, is it not, sir?' Mr. Carrington gestured with a wave of his hand.

'Yes, indeed. But I plan to have it refurbished all the same. Uncle Charles' taste was a bit eccentric.'

'It reminds me of a museum instead of a home.' Miriah observed as she scanned the great hall. A prickly sensation surged up the back of her neck. She turned with deliberate slowness to find him scrutinizing her with a hopeful glint in his eyes.

Lord Rashley cleared his throat and abruptly turned toward her mother. 'Come, my family awaits in the drawing room.' He extended his arm to Mrs. Carrington and escorted her through a set of double doors. Miriah smoothed the folds of her white muslin overskirt as she followed Ann and her father.

The drawing room was more cozy than the grand hall. A pair of sofas sat across from each other in front of a large fireplace. Two ladies sitting side by side stood with the gentlemen who turned at the Carringtons' entrance.

Rashley introduced a blond-haired man as his half brother, Lord Joseph Rashley, the baron, and the shorter lady dressed in a shimmery rose sarcenet dress, as Lady Rashley. Miriah noticed the baron had hazel eyes. The half brothers were similar in their lean frames, except the scar along Garrett's jaw-line enhanced his handsome features with a slight ruggedness that she found appealing.

Next, Lord and Lady Moreland came forward. Rashley's half sister looked more like his lordship. Her hair was a darker shade of brown than the baroness. A British net frock covered the bishop's blue satin slip she wore. The short waist of the dress was ornamented in the French style with a row of lace at the bottom. Her necklace of sapphires brought out the blue in her eyes.

Both women smiled warmly at her. Lady Rashley took Miriah's hand in her dainty one and squeezed it.

'I'm delighted to make your acquaintance, Miss Carrington. We have heard nothing but good things about you.' Lady Rashley's voice was light, feathery and melodic, much like her dress adorned with blond lace at the hem.

Miriah blushed and laughed as she did when she was nervous, along with her chattering. She realized she knew nothing about the two ladies except their names. Perhaps, had she given him the chance the other day, Garrett would have told her more about them.

'Here, sit beside me,' Lady Rashley offered, patting a plump cushion.

Miriah joined her on the sofa and looked up to see Lady Moreland offer her mother and sister a seat on the other sofa.

Miriah turned and asked Lady Rashley. 'How was your journey to Finchston Hall?'

'It was quite jarring from the ruts left in the road by the recent rains. The children took enjoyment in the bumps.

We have three sons, you know.'

'What are their names and ages, Lady Rashley?' Miriah inquired with another nervous laugh. Asking questions was one way to keep herself from chatting.

'Jonathan, the eldest, is ten; then Jacob is eight; and our youngest, Jared, is seven. The boys adore their Uncle Garrett. They like his tales of growing up with their father and, of course, any war stories that are safe enough for their ears.' Lady Rashley paused a moment then added, 'Do you play the pianoforte, Miss Carrington?'

'Yes, I do, a little.'

'And who are your favorite composers?' Lady Rashley's warm smile put her at ease.

'Haydn is my favorite. But I like Mozart, Handel and Giordani.' Miriah liked Lady Rashley for her unaffected manner. She appeared both genuine and sincere.

'Oh, you like Italian too? So do I. Do you prefer the classicals or ballads?'

'Ballads.' It was hard for Miriah to

keep her answers short but she did not want to give Lord Rashley a disgust of her. She'd done that well enough two days ago.

'They tend to be more romantic, I think.' Lady Rashley's smile broadened.

'Yes, yes they do.' Miriah caught herself glancing over Lady Rashley's shoulder at a pair of sharp and assessing sky-blue eyes.

A servant entered the room and announced dinner.

Lord Rashley stepped over to the sofa and offered his arm to his sister-in-law, the highest lady of rank. A knot tightened in Miriah's stomach as she watched him lead the procession through the door. Was this meeting with his family another test of sorts? From the way his eyes strayed to her she didn't know whether he was guarding his emotions in front of the others or waiting to catch her in a faux pas. With her father and Ann, she followed the others out of the drawing room with uncertainty in her heart.

Flames glinted from wall sconces along the dining hall. The table was ornately set with a pair of many-armed candlesticks equally spaced down the center of the mahogany table. A prism of color reflected off the silverware and crystal from the wax tapers. Two ornamental fruit displays sat on either side of the candelabras. Miriah found herself seated between the baron and Lord Moreland. At the head of the table, Lord Rashley conversed amiably with her mother, who sat to one side of him.

'Miss Miriah Carrington.' The baron smiled at her. 'I cannot tell you how delighted I am to make your acquaintance at last. Garrett has spoken highly of you. It seems you have left a prodigious impression on him.'

'I scarce know what to say.' A short nervous laugh escaped her at the baron's kind words.

'I hope we can become better acquainted in time.' A warm smile grew on the baron's face and she began to relax.

Lord Moreland cleared his throat and she turned in his direction.

'I understand that you have been assisting your uncle at his parsonage in Swithingham. You are fortunate that it is very close to Finchstonbury.'

'Yes, I am. But he has found a housekeeper and I have happily returned to the familiarity of home.'

'I dare say it is more convenient for . . . for you to be near your parents.' He laughed hesitantly then turned to the first course the servants placed on the table.

What did he mean by her being near and convenient? Yet, he didn't voice what he had started to say. A familiar warmth burned her cheeks as a possible meaning presented itself. Could he have meant that she was convenient for Lord Rashley to pay calls?

Lord Rashley's melodic laugh caught her attention and she glanced at the head of the table. She took the opportunity to study his profile. Medium brown curls fell casually over his high forehead. His eyebrows reminded her of bird's wings over a straight aquiline nose. Prominent cheekbones that tapered to a narrow oval chin revealed the lengthwise scar that intrigued her.

Miriah raised her gaze to find him watching her. There was a faint glint of humor in his eyes. Then he winked. So he wasn't indifferent to her after all. Relief washed over her and the tension in her shoulders subsided. Lifting a fork to her lips, she tasted the creamed asparagus as she watched the amiable exchange between him and his half brother.

After the servants removed the fish course, she slanted him another look to find him sipping his drink and listening to the baroness, who sat to his right. Miriah took a frank and admiring look at Lord Rashley. His tanned skin reflected his enjoyment of outdoor pursuits, like hunting and riding. While on their first outdoor walk he had mentioned that he took pleasure in fishing.

He carried himself with a commanding air of self-confidence with his high pointed white collar and starched cravat. He was the handsomest man she had ever seen. Of course, she did consider herself prejudiced in her regard for him. Even though she had never been to London, she ventured a guess that he surely outshone any man in the city as well.

A set of blue eyes caught and held her gaze. Warmth stole over her skin and a bevy of butterflies fluttered through her body. He smiled and turned away to answer a question put to him by her mother. She was not sure who spoke, her thoughts were solely on him.

★   ★   ★

Garrett took a bite of ham as his gaze turned to a particular female guest again. He couldn't believe the change that had come over Miriah. Her conversation was precise and she didn't rattle on as she had done two days ago. Yet he knew she must be nervous. On several occasions this evening he heard her skittish little laugh. Another of her mannerisms when she was anxious, he had noticed since meeting her.

Despite his every desire that he should not find Miriah appealing, she was. He took in her petite and flower-like figure in the cream muslin dress with green leaves along the sleeves and hem. If this evening was any indication, he could live easily with her for the rest of his life and even enjoy her company.

'I understand that you served in the Peninsula, Lord Rashley.' Mrs. Carrington drew his attention away from Miriah.

'Yes. I was in the Light Dragoons. I sold my commission less than three months ago.'

'I see. And how many served under you?' Mrs. Carrington showed a genuine interest that reminded him of Miriah.

'Eighty-five soldiers, Madam.'

Mrs. Carrington inquired if he happened to recall meeting a neighbor's son she knew. Then she was drawn to Abigail's opinion on a book she had just read.

Taking the opportunity, Garrett glanced down the table again. He watched the animated gestures of Miriah's hands and sparkling blue-gray eyes as she spoke to Joseph who hung on her every word. Yes, she was more at ease now. When she broadened her smile he noticed her full lips that reminded him of their kiss. Ah, the kiss. It touched him like no other kiss had done before.

A servant reached for Garrett's empty dessert dish and broke his contemplation. Lady Rashley signaled the ladies to leave the gentlemen to their port. The room was not as warm once the ladies departed.

Garrett led the conversation toward hunting and fishing.

'I would like to extend an invitation

to you all,' Mr. Carrington gestured to include Joseph and Samuel along with Garrett, continuing, 'to join me in fishing in the river that runs through my place. I will be happy to furnish you rods and tackle.'

'How kind of you. I'm sure I will have to refurbish the sporting supplies. Uncle had not fished in years and I was probably the last person to use the old stuff a year or so before I bought my commission.' Garrett turned to the other two men. 'Are either of you interested in fishing?'

'Of course.' Joseph beamed.

'If I can talk Abby into staying on an extra day, I wouldn't mind joining you.'

'Surely the ladies will be amiable to the idea if they are given the chance to visit the local shops as we pursue our sporting pleasures,' Garrett suggested, before turning to Samuel and adding, 'Do you think Abigail will be inclined to stay for a shopping expedition?'

'Of course, Gar,' Samuel agreed.

Before long, the men concluded their

plans and rose to join the ladies in the blue salon. Jennifer and Miriah, their heads bent together in conversation as they sat on a sofa, looked up. It surprised Garrett that his sister-in-law would form a fast friendship with Miriah. She had always seemed rather picky in who she befriended. It warmed his heart to know his family accepted her. He just did not expect friendships could form so quick.

On the other hand, he noticed Miss Carrington sitting meekly beside her mother. She had not spoken more than half a dozen words all evening. He crossed the room toward Abigail, Mrs. Carrington and Miss Carrington.

'Miss Carrington. Did you enjoy dinner?' Taking a seat in a chair beside hers, he saw Miriah smiling in approval at the attention he paid to her sister.

'Y . . . yes, my lord. Thank you.' Miss Carrington looked flustered.

'What did you like best about the meal? Cook is always fishing for compliments.'

'Oh.' Miss Carrington looked pensive. 'I especially liked the strawberry flan. The venison was excellent.'

Garrett smiled at her in hopes that she would feel more at ease. 'Do you by any chance, play the pianoforte?'

'Wh . . . why yes. But not very well, my lord.' Her hand went up to her bosom.

He guessed her answer before he asked, but he had to inquire before he asked the other ladies to play. 'Would you by any chance play for us this evening? I would very much like to hear you play.'

'I . . . uh . . . M . . . Miriah is more at ease playing in front of an audience than I am, my lord. Please. I play very poorly in front of others.'

'I will not force you, Miss Carrington. It is just that I wished you to have an opportunity to play if you had the desire to do so. I would wager you have a fine ear for music.'

She offered a half smile as she cast her eyes in a demure fashion to her lap.

'Perhaps we can sit here together and listen to the other ladies play.' Surely she spoke to her betrothed. It would be a great pity never to speak one's mind. Her sister definitely had no trouble doing so.

As if on cue, Jennifer strolled to the pianoforte, pulled out a sheet of music, and began to tickle the ivories.

'Are you familiar with that particular piece, Miss Carrington?'

'Yes. It is Handel.'

'Ah, I believe you are correct.' He listened intently at the staccato rhythm of church music he had not heard in years.

After playing two selections, Jennifer rose and invited Miriah to take her seat at the instrument. As Miriah replaced the baroness at the pianoforte, she glanced across the room at Garrett and he smiled. It took her a couple of minutes to find a selection. Then her fingers moved slowly across the keys in a haunting melody.

'That, my lord, is one of her favorite

ballads.' Miss Carrington's soft voice surprised him. She anticipated his question. He looked over at her and saw what must be pride shining in her eyes. A semblance of a smile grew on her upturned lips and she tilted her head as she studied her sister.

Garrett turned to watch Miriah. She had a sweet, clear voice and she articulated beautifully. He could imagine her singing to a baby and it falling asleep in her arms. He drew in a deep breath as he observed the elegance of her posture at the pianoforte. In future he could envision himself relaxing after dinner while she played for him alone.

Out of the corner of his eye he noticed Miss Carrington observing him. Could she know what he was thinking? Did she have a sixth sense like Miriah?

'She plays very well indeed.' Garrett watched the shadows of emotion on Miriah's face as she lulled the audience with romantic lyrics.

'My sister has the voice of a Skylark.

Do you not agree, my lord?' She whispered.

'I concur. If she just did not chatter aimlessly.' He could have bit his tongue. Why did he speak of what annoyed him about Miriah with her sister when she had controlled the habit so well this evening? Perhaps Miss Carrington had the good sense not to relate his stupid remark.

'She only speaks so when she is anxious. The more comfortable she is with you the less inclined she will be to prattle, my lord. Please, give her the benefit of the doubt.'

He glanced at Miss Carrington. 'Wise words coming from a lady who rarely speaks. I am deeply honored that you chose to speak this evening.' His voice was barely above a whisper, as was hers. She smiled once more, and he returned it. Strange as it did seem, he had made a friend with the one lady who rarely bestowed her thoughts on anyone.

Miriah stopped singing and Garrett

applauded with the others. Next she played a selection from one of the masters.

'Mozart, my lord. 'Fantasy in D Minor'.' Miss Ann leaned over to whisper again.

He said nothing but sat mesmerized by the emotion engendered by Miriah's hands gliding over the keys. It was a short selection, but it was beautiful. Miriah stood to return to her seat.

'Do play another selection, Miss Miriah,' Abigail insisted.

'Oh, but it is your turn, my lady. I would not think of monopolizing the pianoforte.'

'But I have not played in an age and I am quite sure that I have grown rusty. Please play another selection, I insist.'

'My wife speaks the truth. I quite agree that you should favor us with another piece.' Lord Moreland looked about the room. 'Do you not all agree?'

'Of course. Please. Another Mozart perhaps?' Garrett waved his hand toward the pianoforte, then glanced at

Abigail. Surely she could not mean that she had grown rusty. Did she realize Miriah played with the same intensity as herself?

Slowly, Miriah took her seat. Without a music sheet she played.

He spoke in a hushed tone to her sister. 'This one I do know, Miss Carrington. Symphony 29.'

'Very good, my lord.'

Eyes forward, he never wavered from the pianist. She played with a great passion, evoking a powerful emotion that darkened her eyes to slate.

When Miriah lifted her fingers at the finale, she stood and regained her seat beside Jennifer. He kept his gaze on her, but she would not look over at him. Yet, her cheeks held a rose-colored blush. She knew he was observing her. It warmed his heart and pleased him to know he could inspire sentiment in her.

'My lord. Will your family be present at the next assembly in the village?' Mrs. Carrington inquired of him.

'I had not thought of it. I presume we

shall.' Garrett had not wanted to go since he was not keen on social gatherings, but he was sure that Abigail and Jennifer would insist on going if the Carringtons were planning to attend.

'Oh, yes, Garrett. We must. It has been ten months since Uncle Charles' passing and we are out of mourning now. The village folk will think it uncivil of us if we do not put in an appearance.' Lady Jennifer offered. 'Is your family attending, Mrs. Carrington?'

'Of course we are. And it would be most pleasing to the families hereabout to visit with you.' Mrs. Carrington waved a hand to include them all.

When Abigail and Jennifer looked his way, he could not say no. 'It is settled then. We shall be present.'

5

Later that night, Garrett lay awake staring through the darkness at the canopy above his bed. The music of Mozart still played in his mind. Closing his eyes, he visualized a certain blond-haired beauty whose thick curls fell loose about her shoulders. Her willowy figure walking out of a grove of trees showed to perfection as a breeze blew the folds of her silk dress. The color in her face was heightened by the exertion of walking.

Then he recalled her poise earlier that evening. He admired her talent as she gracefully played the pianoforte, and he had to admit she had a fine voice.

But a talented lady was still a female. Was she as sincere as she appeared or merely play-acting as Dorothea had done over two years ago? What it boiled down to was that he didn't trust his own judgement where females were concerned. And yet, his family reacted with warmth toward her they hadn't shown to Dorothea. They accepted her. Why couldn't he decide, if she was as genuine as she appeared?

With a heavy sigh, he rolled over and muttered to the darkness, 'Leave me in peace, Miriah. I want to sleep.' He closed his eyes without losing the vision of her.

Morning came early. And the memory of Miriah lingered on his mind. Pushing himself out of bed, he shuffled to the closed window. Reaching up, he pulled the thick curtain to one side. The sun had not crested the trees. A good gallop was what he needed to clear the cobwebs out of his head. He regretted making plans to ride with Joseph and Samuel this morning. A solitary ride would restore his sense of freedom for a little while.

'Mornin' your lordship.' Denby

stepped into the bedroom and greeted his master.

'Have Danté saddled, please, Denby.' Garrett dropped the curtain on the early morning sky, but not on the blue-gray eyes that lingered in his mind. He crossed to his dressing room.

Stepping down the stairs half an hour later, he headed for the dining room and found it vacant. He drew his watch out of the fob pocket and flipped it open. Twelve minutes to the hour and the appointed time the other two men were to meet him. A footman came out of a side door.

'Coffee, please.' Garrett pulled a chair from the table. The servant returned shortly with a steaming cup of brew. Between sips, Garrett checked the time. They had two minutes in which to walk through the door. His fingers drummed a monotonous beat on the table. He glanced at the timepiece in his hand. Eight of the o'clock. The only sound came from a log spitting fire up the chimney. Lack of punctuality had been a source of irritation since his salad days.

'That settles it. I will ride alone.' He muttered in a low voice to himself before he stepped out into the hallway and headed for a rear door. Perhaps Joseph and Samuel had changed their minds about the ride after all.

A slight breeze whisked against his skin as he pressed Danté to a gallop. Over the lush hill and down the valley he raced the Thoroughbred toward the river, then guided him along the ridge above the bank of the meandering stream. The trees were a blur of green and brown as he spirited Danté past them. Birds darted out of the branches of low hanging limbs at the thunderous sound of hooves against the earth.

Peace and quiet as he knew it would come to an end with marriage. Especially to Miriah. But she had done well last night with just enough conversation. Her mother must have taken her to task after his last visit to the Carringtons. Whatever Mrs. Carrington did, he hoped Miriah could continue her new reticence. Could she have been looking to him for his approval last evening? If so, her desire to please him touched a cord in his heart.

An hour and a half later, Garrett walked into the breakfast parlor to be met by Abigail and Jennifer.

'Did you enjoy your morning ride, Garrett?' Abigail lowered her cup to the table.

'Of course. As I usually do.'

The smile on Jen's face widened. 'I thought last evening's dinner party was a success. The Carringtons are nice people.' She took a bite of toast covered with a generous helping of strawberry jam.

'Yes. I thought all went well.' He reached for a plate off the sideboard, filling it with kippers and eggs.

'Miss Miriah Carrington's musical ability was astonishing. Was it not, brother?' Abigail studied him with a keen eye as he sat down beside her.

'Yes, it was. She is an accomplished pianist. Her sister regaled me with the title to each piece Miss Miriah Carrington played and appeared extremely proud of her sister.' He shoveled a fork full of eggs into his mouth. It appeared he was not to have any peace from Miriah by the sound of the conversation. Not that that was a bad thing. Part of him wanted to hear more about her.

'Miss Carrington spoke to you? I barely heard her say two words all evening.' Surprise tinged Jennifer's voice as she stared wide-eyed at him.

'That is why I sat near her, to draw her out.' Garrett was compelled to answer. 'She is engaged and I cannot imagine how that came about unless it is an arranged marriage. I wonder if the young man, if he is young, has even met her? If she cannot speak in small company, how is she to speak to her betrothed after they are married?' He tipped his coffee cup up. 'It would do Miss Carrington good to emulate her younger sister more, as she did last evening.'

A servant slipped into the room, refilled Garrett's cup and replaced the empty pot on the sideboard then departed the room.

'I did not get the impression that Miss Miriah Carrington is a talker, and I sat next to her most of the time.' Jennifer raised an eyebrow.

'She was unusually quiet last evening. I feel it was her mother's doing.'

'Yes, Joseph mentioned you found her to be a chatterbox. One would hope, if the dinner party was any indication, that she could change.' Abigail laid her fork on her plate. 'I must say, I was very impressed with her. She carried herself well and did not seem to put on airs or flirt with the men folk like some young girls are wont to do. She seemed most pleasing.'

'We have plans to go into the village this afternoon, Miss Miriah Carrington and I. You do not mind, do you, Garrett?' Jen's brow wrinkled under his scrutiny.

'You are becoming fast friends.' He didn't expect Jennifer to open her arms so easily to Miriah, though the idea did cross his mind of the lady encircled in his arms.

'And why not, may I inquire? She is amiable.' His sister-in-law defended.

'I did not say she wasn't. It is just that I did not expect you to become bosom bows so quickly, that is all.' He stuck a fork of pickled herring into his mouth, none too gently, then followed the tart fish with a sip of coffee.

'If it displeases you, I shall send my regrets, Garrett.'

'No. I did not say it displeased me. You misunderstand.' With a slice of toast in one hand, he pushed the eggs off his plate onto the fork. Jennifer's words confused him to the point of ill manners.

'Do I?'

'Yes. I am happy for you to become friends. I simply did not expect it so soon.' Garrett rushed the fork full of eggs to his mouth, chewed briefly and swallowed. 'Please. Go to the village with her and enjoy yourself. I implore you.'

Jennifer merely stared at him for a long moment then went back to eating her eggs and jam covered toast.

'I understand she is a lady of faith. What do you think of that, Gar?' Abigail eyed him across the table.

'I do not mind as long as she does not impose her faith on me.'

'I feel she will be a good influence on you.' His half sister smiled, but he saw a challenge in her eyes.

'Don't you fear I will be a bad influence on her?'

'Not necessarily. Do you suppose your uncle chose her to be your bride because of her strong faith?'

He froze. After a long pause he spoke in a low monotone. 'What does faith have to do with my marriage?'

'Perhaps you did not realize. Your Uncle Charles had a religious conversion a year before he died. I have a feeling he wanted you to accept God as he had done, but not wait until you are near death to do it.'

'I repeat. What has faith to do with my marriage, Abigail?'

'I do not know. You will have to find that out for yourself.' She picked up her cup and sipped tea, keeping her gaze on him as she did so. He resented her suggestion and found his half sister's attention very disconcerting.

After a slight pause, Jennifer spoke. 'I noticed most of your attention was spent on the eldest Miss Carrington. She is already spoken for, is she not? And your conversation with Miss Miriah Carrington was very minimal.'

'You are correct on both counts.' He stared at his plate as he answered her. 'One can learn much from simple observation — and paying attention to what others say about the person being scrutinized. Do you not agree?'

'Your penchant for observing an interested *parti* escaped my memory. You are very clever, indeed.' Jennifer's eyes twinkled with amusement as she tilted her head.

Male voices were heard before the door swung open to reveal Garrett's half brother and brother-in-law entering the breakfast parlour.

'Ah-ha. You evaded us this bright morning by twenty minutes. Joseph and I had hoped to catch up to you but it is obvious we took the wrong direction from the stables.' Samuel leaned over and planted a kiss on Abigail's cheek.

'I told you both the precise time I planned to ride.' Garrett spoke in a disinterested voice. 'You did not show up, so I presumed you had changed your minds about riding out this morning.'

'You have always been punctual, Garrett.' Samuel poured himself a cup of coffee. 'And I must say I admire you for that. But there are times when it is fashionable to be late.'

'Jared was positively late when he was born. Do you not agree, Joseph?' Jennifer chimed in regards to their youngest son.

'Yes, dearest.' Joseph glanced back at Garrett. 'What will you do if your offspring chooses to wait three weeks after he is expected? Discipline him? I hardly think so.'

'If he is of my blood, he cannot help but be punctual.'

'What if you have a daughter?' Jennifer interjected.

'Excuse me. Are you not putting the cart before the horse? I need a wife to beget these infants before you start to press me about their upbringing.' He leveled a look at Joseph and Samuel and deftly changed the subject. 'Are either of you in a mood for bird hunting today? I dare say the weather is perfect for it.'

An hour later, Joseph and Samuel joined Garrett on the far side of the stables. A gust of wind ruffled the treetops with a swishing sound. Frogs croaked from the stream that meandered down the gentle rolling hill.

The gamekeeper led them beyond the birch and oak trees down the slope

139

where grass reached Garrett's knees. In front of him, two servants beat the tall blades with narrow wooden paddles to flush out the quail.

The sudden whir of wings as the birds darted up from their hiding place in front of him quickened the beat of his heart. He raised the barrel of his shotgun, aimed and fired. One of the small birds fell to the ground.

It had been four years since Garrett had the pleasure of hunting with Joseph and Samuel. With relief, he enjoyed the physical pursuit that required no thoughts of marriage.

★ ★ ★

'Ann, why did you tell such a taradiddle to Lord Rashley last evening? You are accomplished at the pianoforte, more so than I.' Miriah sat close to Ann and reached for her embroidery from the box next to her chair. 'Your penchant for committing music to memory is astonishing.'

'It is easier to play from memory than it is to play in front of strangers. It does not suit me to be the center of attention.'

Miriah was moved to say. 'But it is not such a hardship to play before a small group. You could have tried.'

'Miriah.' Ann sighed.

'One day, you shall have the confidence to play and talk easily with others.' Miriah didn't mind sharing her feelings with Ann with regards to matters of the heart. For Ann came to her for advice when Mr. Sumner first courted her before she became betrothed. The kind Mr. Sumner showed an open admiration for Ann from their first meeting. 'Speaking of which, I noticed you conversing with Lord Rashley. Whatever did he say to draw you into a tête-à-tête with him?'

A cloud of unease passed over her at the picture of Lord Rashley's head bent toward her sister. Just as quickly she checked her emotion when she remembered the look in Lord Rashley's blue eyes across the salon. His warm smile made her heart sing with delight.

'We were merely discussing the composers for each piece of music Lady Rashley and you played.' Ann tilted her head to the side, her gaze not fixed on anything in particular. 'I do not know how he did it, but he drew me into the discussion, however brief it was, quite easily.'

'Splendid.' The viscount exhibited more forbearance than she gave him credit for. His generous show of caring brought a smile to her lips. 'He did what Mr. Sumner took months to do and he became betrothed to you even before you spoke two words in his presence.'

'John, I mean Mr. Sumner, is very patient with me. Besides, it took me three months to know that he understood my shyness. I have since learned we share many things in common, like a love of music for one.'

'How wonderful for you, Ann. I am glad Mr. Sumner holds a special place in your heart. The two of you are well suited to one another. You are so blessed.' Miriah patted her sister's hand. 'I hope that I will one day find myself betrothed to an understanding and patient man like you.'

'I have the feeling you will before long, sister dear.'

Ann returned Miriah's smile. 'Which dress are you wearing to the assembly this evening?'

★ ★ ★

Thomas Ottley, known as Ott since school at Eaton, arrived as Garrett came in from hunting earlier. 'What good fortune to be a second son and still inherit, even though it is not your natural home but your uncle's.'

'You forget one small detail, Ott. I must marry before it is rightfully mine. And not just any lady.' Garrett leaned his head back against the tufted squabs of his carriage. He could hear the sound of Joseph's coach following them and breathed a sigh of relief that there was not enough room for him and Ottley to ride with the other two couples.

'Ah, yes. And is she hatchet faced? Or is she pleasing to the eye?' Ottley raised an eyebrow and waited for his reply.

'Miss Miriah Carrington is a fine looking young lady.'

'I note a certain reserve in your voice, old boy. What is the complaint against her?' Knowing Ottley as an astute observer of human nature, his query was no surprise to Garrett.

'She has a propensity to chatter when excited or nervous. And you know me, Ott. I prefer a more composed companion.'

'Yes, you never did like ladies, or gentlemen for that matter, who like to hear themselves talk and never take the time to listen.'

'She listens.'

'I see.' Ottley fell silent and studied him across the carriage.

The fashionable drag slowed and Garrett peered out the window. Oil lamps illuminated the front of the assembly room in the village inn where patrons filed in the front door. His fingers tapped against his thigh as the carriage inched its way nearer the entry. The drone of people chatting inconsequential drivel as they shuffled inside made him long for the solitude of his study. He disliked standing around and making small talk at crowded functions.

The carriage door swung open and the footman lowered the step. Lord Rashley stepped down, followed by Ottley. Moving out of the way, he waited for the second carriage to pull up.

'It appears we are not the only early arrivals.' Abigail climbed down, then came to stand by Garrett and his friend.

'We are not early, merely on time.' He spoke without looking in her direction, then proceeded up the steps. Two liveried servants stood on either side of the wide door.

Ladies and gentlemen stood in small

groups exchanging pleasantries, from the sound of their conversation. Garrett scanned the candle-lit room. On the far side, near a tall potted plant, stood Miss Miriah Carrington in close conversation with a willowy brown-haired young woman: Miriah caught his eye and smiled pleasingly at him. His stomach turned a somersault.

'Ott, come with me and I shall introduce you to Miss Miriah Carrington.' Making his way across the room, he took in her appearance from the tip of her blond curls pulled softly back, to the blush-colored dress that enhanced the hue of her fair skin. His gaze moved back up to her blue-gray eyes, sparkling in the light of the many candles along the walls.

'Miss Miriah Carrington.' Garrett bowed and admired more closely her figure in the gauzy material that fell from her highwaisted dress. 'May I request your hand for the first country dance?'

'Yes, my lord.' The warmth of her

smile echoed in her voice.

'Will you present me to your friend?' He looked more closely at the girl who stood a half head taller than Miss Miriah Carrington. She was not what he would call a beauty, but she was handsome. Her hazel eyes did not waver from his level look.

'Miss Hanbury, may I present Lord Rashley who is living at his uncle's estate Finchston Park.'

'Pleased to make your acquaintance, my lord.' Catherine Hanbury curtsied. 'When last you were here over four years ago, I believe, I had been away visiting relatives in the north.'

'Allow me to procure the second set with you then, if I may? In that way we shall have remedied the omission of not meeting on my last visit to my uncle's.'

'Thank you, my lord. But I am promised for the second set.'

'Then may I have the third.'

'Very well, my lord.' She lavished a smile on him.

Ottley cleared his throat and Garrett

glanced back in surprise before turning once more to the ladies. 'Oh, I quite forgot. May I present my friend, Mr. Ottley. Thomas, may I introduce Miss Miriah Carrington and Miss Hanbury.'

After nodding to Miriah, Thomas addressed her friend. 'Would you do me the honour, Miss Hanbury, for the first set?'

'Of course, sir.'

Thomas bowed and turned to Miriah and solicited her hand for a dance.

The thought of Miriah dancing with another man vaguely disturbed Garrett. After accepting Ott's offer to dance, she turned her dazzling countenance back to him. A forced smile, and his pride, concealed his inner turmoil. Ott was doing the pretty by requesting Miriah's hand, and Miss Hanbury's he belatedly reminded himself. Nothing havy-cavy here.

In a short time, the musicians began to warm up their instruments. Garrett offered his hand to Miriah and led her onto the dance floor. Ottley, likewise, escorted Miss Hanbury.

Garrett stood facing Miriah in line with the other couples and waited for the music to start. He noticed the small gold cross that hung above her square neckline. Garnets adorned the pendant resting against her smooth skin.

He looked up to see the warmth in her eyes and smiled reassuringly at her. Yes. She would make a beautiful wife. Maybe, in time, he could even come to trust her the way he trusted Abigail and Jennifer.

'My lord, permit me to thank you for the lovely dinner last evening. My family and I most heartily enjoyed meeting your half brother and sister and their spouses.'

The steps to the dance separated them briefly.

'I wish to compliment you on your expertise on the pianoforte. You play superbly.'

She blushed prettily and lowered her gaze.

'May I thank you for talking to Ann

as you did?' They stood apart while another couple swung around in front of them. Coming together again, he smiled and she added, 'It is a rare talent indeed to draw more than two words from her. She is extremely shy.'

'I have noticed,' he said before letting go of her hand. 'Does she speak easily with her betrothed?'

'It took all of three months.'

'Three months. And he still asked for her hand?'

Another couple circled in front of them, cutting the conversation briefly.

'But of course, he loved her, do you not see? It mattered not if she spoke a word, Mr. Sumner said. He had faith that she would eventually start talking and never stop.' She smiled and nodded for emphasis.

He could only laugh at her words.

The dance came to an end, but she continued to talk. 'He said that it was his belief that Ann never spoke because I did all the talking for her. Can you believe that?'

'Incredible.' He eyed her suspiciously as she chatted on about her sister. She didn't appear nervous to him as he led her off the dance floor. From the tail of his eye he saw Ott walking Miss Hanbury to the far side of the room.

'What is it, my lord?' She tilted her head, looking thoughtful. 'I have the feeling you wish to say that I might learn from her example of silence.'

'Now, why would I say such a thing?'

'You have mentioned it before. When you first came to call. Remember?' The smile had faded on her face.

'Ah, yes. I do recall my unfortunate utterance. Perhaps I did not mean for you to take my words so seriously.'

'I am not so foolish as to ignore my tendency to talk overmuch on occasion. You do not need to mince words with me on that matter. My eyes do not lie to me when I see gentlemen turn away after one dance and never return. I talk them into boredom, I know.'

'Miss Miriah Carrington. Let me tell you how proud I am of your control last evening. May I point out that you chatter a trifle too much when uneasy, perhaps, but you are mastering even that tendency.' His voice was low. As he communicated his feelings to her, he noticed her eyes glisten with the hint of unshed tears. 'Are you feeling ill?'

'No my lord.' She whispered and her lips twisted up on one side in a half smile. 'I am . . . I am pleased at such kind words.'

Touched at her pleasure in so small approval, and resentful that she has been given so little of it, he wanted nothing more than to help her think better of herself in future.

'May I fetch you some liquid refreshment?' He led her to a chair at the side of the room.

'Punch would be welcome. It is becoming dreadfully warm in here.' Pulling a fan out of her reticule, she drew it open. After a low bow, he turned back to the refreshment table.

Ottley came up beside him as Garrett filled two glasses.

'This may be an interesting evening after all, old boy. You completely forgot my existence simply by standing before her.' He grinned.

Over Ottley's shoulder, Garrett caught sight of another familiar face. 'Oh, no.' He groaned. 'Ott, I need your help. There is another female present with black hair and hazel eyes. I need you to occupy her as best you can. She is across the room behind you.'

Ottley turned around casually, glancing across the room. 'The one looking away from the older, stout lady?'

'The very one. Her name is Miss Sneed. Here she comes. She is very bold.'

'Lord Rashley, fancy meeting you here. I thought you had returned to London,' she gushed.

'No, I have not gone back to London at all.' He glanced over at Ottley. 'By the way, may I present Mr. Ottley to you, Miss Sneed?'

Ottley took over and asked Miss Sneed for the dance that was just

153

beginning. Garrett sighed a breath of relief and returned to Miriah's side with refreshment. They sat the dance out and made light conversation about the assembly and the weather. When Miss Hanbury returned from the last dance, Garrett immediately stood up with her. Mr. Emrick who had returned with Miss Hanbury requested Miriah's hand for the quadrille and the two couples completed a set.

It was obvious to Garrett that Miriah and Mr. Emrick were friends of some standing. Conversation was easy between them and less formal, without any inclination to nervous chatter on her part. He guessed Miss Hanbury was equally associated with Mr. Emrick, for her eyes strayed to him when she should have been looking at Garrett. Perhaps there was more than friendship in that quarter.

While dancing his gaze encountered Miss Sneed's as she craned her neck in his direction. She pursed her lips in a pouty smile. If he did not miss the mark, she intended to dance with him before the night was out.

Where was Ottley? He looked about the crowded room to find Ottley dancing with Jennifer. The music came to an end and he bowed slightly to his partner.

'Thank you for the dance, Miss Hanbury. You are very light on your feet.' He reached for Miriah's hand while releasing Miss Hanbury over to Mr. Emrick. 'Miss Miriah Carrington, I believe the next dance is promised to me. Is it not?'

'Why . . . yes, if you say so.' She looked a mixture of confusion and surprise. The dance was a country dance.

He didn't have to look over to know that Miss Sneed had maneuvered her partner to stand on the other side of Miss Hanbury and Mr. Emrick. He felt irritated that she had the audacity to draw his attention when it should have been apparent to her that he wanted no part of her. Before long, Miriah's gaze fell on Miss Sneed. She forced a smile when she looked back at him.

'I believe you have not danced with Miss Sneed this evening, my lord.'

'No. I have not.' It did not surprise him that Miriah noticed his omission with Miss Sneed. He hoped she did not inquire why he did not dance with the lady. He did not wish to explain. It was just that Miss Sneed was sending out lures in his direction. If there were to be any chasing, he preferred to do it himself.

'Perhaps you should. For it is unkind of you to neglect her when she appears to desire a dance with you.' Miriah slanted a look at Miss Sneed.

'How can I put this without sounding discourteous?' He lowered his voice when she came near in the dance. 'She appears somewhat bold, and I cannot respect a lady for being so presumptuous.'

'My lord, have you never heard of Christian charity? You must be familiar with the term. After all, you are dancing with me a second time, which is an exception in itself. But I do not read anything into it other than a kindness you are bestowing on me. After all. I did confess my plight to you earlier this evening with regard to my misfortune of excessive talking.' She continued after the separation during the dance. 'Why, it is the same thing with her. She cannot help her nature of appearing forward anymore than I can help rambling on, as I am doing yet again. What I am trying to say is, that it would be to your advantage to show kindness to every lady, my lord, regardless of what flaw she may have in her character. Do you not agree?'

'I think I understand what you are saying. But I did not equate dancing with you a second time as Christian charity. It was solely my pleasure to do so.' He hoped she believed him, for it was the truth. When the dance ended, he returned her to her mother's side and bowed slightly. 'Thank you for the dance and enlightening me with your thoughtful words.'

He turned and marched to where Miss Sneed stood conversing with her last partner. All the while, Miriah's words that he danced with her out of charity, touched a cord in his heart. Did she honestly think that? How could she misconstrue his attentions? Come to think of it, how did a slip of a girl have the power to talk him into doing that which he did not desire to do? Perhaps she would see by his actions that he wanted to please her. She might conclude that his regard for her was indeed sincere and not charity as she assumed.

Reaching the dark haired lady, Garrett bowed and requested her hand for the dance starting up. Leading her out onto the floor, he did his duty, or by Miriah's words, Christian charity.

'Lord Rashley.' When the dance had come to an end, Miss Sneed began to fan herself with her hand. 'I do believe I feel quite warm.'

'May I get you a glass of punch, perhaps?'

'Thank you, no. I will feel more the thing if I could get some fresh air.' She flicked a pearl stemmed fan open.

On closer inspection he noticed she did look very pale all of a sudden. Perhaps she was becoming ill. Just as quickly the word actress came to mind. Recollection of Dorothea's theatrics flashed before him. He looked back on their courtship and saw the signs that hc was blind to at the time. Like a bell in the fog, he heard it clanging now. Yet, there was nothing he could do about it as she began to lean toward him. 'Allow me to assist you to the balcony.'

Glancing about the room for reinforcements, he found none. Ott was in conversation with Miriah. Neither looked his way. Taking Miss Sneed by the elbow, he led her toward a door that opened onto a balcony. He lowered her to the closest seat against the railing.

Two more couples strolled out of the warm assembly room to take the air.

Looking back into the hall, he saw Ottley lead Miriah out on the dance floor. He wished he had not taken her advice and danced with the dark haired beauty. Look where it got him. Glancing down at her, he studied the lady who made a show of herself. What an actress. If he told her he didn't believe her, he was sure she would make a scene and call attention to them.

After what seemed an eternity, she finally submitted to being led back into the assembly room. He walked with her to her mother and handed her over to the stout lady, then turned on his heels to find Ottley conversing with Miriah again.

'Miss Carrington, are you enjoying the evening?' He inquired when he came to stand beside her.

'Thank you, yes.' Her answer was curt and she would not look him in the eye. Was she put out with him for dancing with Miss Sneed when it was her idea? Perhaps she was angry because he walked Miss Sneed out on the balcony. Yes, that had to be it, though his ending up in that fix could be laid only at her door. He rolled his eyes. As long as he lived, he would not understand the female logic.

Where was Miss Carrington? He had a sudden need to dance with quiet Ann. He looked along the wall of chairs and spotted her sitting alone. Fleetingly he wondered where her betrothed was? Excusing himself, he marched over to the shy sister.

'Miss Carrington, would you do me the honor of the next dance?'

She looked up at him with wide blue eyes. 'Uh . . . uh — '

'I insist that you dance with me. You do know how, do you not?'

'Uh . . . of course, my lord.' Stammering, she slowly put her hand in his. A bright blush covered her cheeks. Her hand shook slightly and he held it firm.

'You do not have to talk if you do not wish it.' That would ease her mind, he thought. She nodded. As they danced he offered her words of encouragement and felt her relax a little.

Looking up, he caught Miriah watching him but she quickly turned her head away. Maybe she thought he danced with Ann to make amends for his actions with Miss Sneed. Well, he did not have to vindicate himself to any woman. He turned his gaze back to Ann and smiled.

At the end of the assembly, Garrett watched Miriah leave with her family. It was just as well that she left. She had turned a cold shoulder on him the remainder of the evening. Perchance he should apologize, but she was the one who literally pushed him to dance with the Sneed flirt. He sighed heavily.

★ ★ ★

'Did Lord Rashley say anything to you while you stood up with him, Ann?' Miriah queried her sister in Ann's room after returning from the assembly. It was not likely, but Garrett might have

162

mentioned to Ann why he took Miss Sneed out on the balcony.

'Nothing of import. He complimented me on my dancing ability, that is all.' Ann looked back at her and tilted her head. 'Why would you not speak to him after he danced with me? Were you jealous that he partnered me? Is that it?'

'No, no. I did not mind him dancing with you. It is just . . . ' It wasn't Ann she was jealous of, but Miss Sneed. Why did she allow Rebecca Sneed to get under her skin? Truth to tell, she feared she would lose Garrett. What was she thinking? Garrett wasn't hers to lose. They were not promised to each other. But it was her desire to be promised to him.

'Just what? I did not see him do anything ungentlemanly.'

'Ann, you do not understand.' Miriah plopped on the side of Ann's bed. 'He took Rebecca Sneed out on the balcony.'

'Yes, I noticed it as well.' Ann sat

163

beside Miriah and patted her clenched hands.

'They stayed there longer than a dance. It was most improper.' She wanted Garrett to dance with Miss Sneed, but she preferred that he return to her side. Was that so unreasonable? It was against her belief to be jealous, but she couldn't help herself at the moment.

'Perhaps he was not the one at fault. We both know Rebecca and it seems highly likely that she contrived to get him alone.' Ann looked at her more closely. 'I did notice several couples stepping out for air at the same time. They were hardly alone.'

'That is not the point. What troubles me is that I insisted that he dance with her. I did not think he would do more than that. And I definitely did not expect him to take her out for fresh air!' The words sounded petty to her own ears. She wanted to cry. If anyone was to blame, it was herself for pushing Garrett into Rebecca's net. And what did she do, but give him the cold shoulder. What must he think of her? She closed her eyes to the horror of her unkindness toward him.

'Miriah, it is unseemly to force a man to do anything. Yet when you do, you must allow him the benefit of the doubt. Why, I am sure he was simply being a gentleman and without any other thought, took her out for some air. It was dreadfully stuffy indoors.' She paused, then added, 'In my eyes he is very much the gentleman. Not many men, and I think there are only two, would have taken the time and patience to talk to me and ask me to dance. I have not danced since Mr. Sumner was last here.' Ann's eyes took on a dream-like quality as she stared into space. 'You know, it has been two months since his mother died. It seems much longer to me.'

'Perhaps you are right, sister dear. It is my fault for making a mountain out of a molehill.' Miriah frowned and slumped her shoulders. Her attachment to Garrett had turned her into a jealous cat, and she didn't like such a negative spirit in herself.

Ann put a thin, bird-like arm on her shoulder. 'Now, off to bed with you. When next you see him, you can make amends. I know which direction the wind blows. You think very highly of him, do you not?'

Miriah merely peered through lowered lashes at her older sister. Smiling, she cradled Ann's hand in hers. Anyone else would think it strange to hear Ann speak so freely. But in the safe environs of home, and in the privacy of her room, she shared most of her deepest thoughts with Miriah. Ann used her shyness to her own advantage and studied people. If anything, she was a very good judge of character. Miriah respected her keen judgement. If Ann trusted Garrett, how could she have believed he would act in an ungentlemanly way?

The following afternoon, Miriah stood gazing out of the parlour window frowning at nothing in particular. Lady Jennifer Rashley had just departed from taking tea with Mrs. Carrington, Ann and herself.

Garrett was not coming. In fact, he had departed at first light with his two male relatives and his friend. They were going to Mr. Ottley's hunting box a two-day journey to the north, specifically 'the shires.'

The burden of guilt weighed her down. What must he think of her? She did her utmost not to give him a disgust of her by her idle chatter, and then showed him an equally damaging side of her character. She forced him to do Christian charity then she denied that same charity to him.

6

Garrett listened to the melody of a small, brown pipit. It ascended in the late afternoon sky on swift-beating wings, then glided slowly downward, filling the glade with its song as it settled on a branch of a birch tree. Danté tossed his head, pulling on the bridle in Garrett's hand.

'Danté's telling me that I am going too slow for him. He does not care for bird watching.' He lead Danté on to a trot and came up beside Ottley's sorrel.

'This is a picturesque ride.' Ottley spoke as he glanced around him. 'After all, we are in no great hurry, are we? No hunting is to be done. Perhaps we shall play billiards in the evenings and fish during the day.'

Ottley led the way up the hill, through the trees.

'You have the right of it. We might as

well slow our pace and take in the tranquility of the River Dove.' Joseph's voice chimed in as his horse cantered alongside Samuel's.

Garrett slowed his pace as he studied the reflection of limbs hanging over the water's edge. Miriah would see this as an opportunity to fish. The corners of his mouth lifted in a grin as he pictured Miriah sitting on a rock with a rod in her hand. Farther downstream, water cascaded over rocky areas below the ponds.

Glancing up the trail, he saw Samuel eyeing him.

'I used to take all this for granted.' Garrett gestured with a wide sweep of his hand. 'Enlisting my services in the Peninsular Wars has changed my attitude. I have seen my share of death and destruction. Give me the rustle of leaves in a soothing whisper above my head instead of cannon fire. And air that smells of birch, beech and oak trees as opposed to acrid smoke.'

Crossing a rock bridge over the

babbling water, Ottley led them up the slope and through a tree-lined path.

Now, the sounds of barking dogs and voices were heard as the site of a small village with its medieval houses on either side of the lane, opened before them. Shutters provided privacy on the ground floor of the half-timbered houses in the evenings and prevented drafts in the winter. To the right sat the larger structure, the Grey Boar Inn.

'We will stay here for the night. It is fairly clean and the food and drink are excellent.' Ottley spoke as he climbed down from his horse.

'It has been a while since we last ate.' Joseph patted his stomach to emphasize his want of food.

Garrett dismounted, put his hands at the small of his back and stretched. 'A bed sounds inviting.'

Stepping through the doorway, he waited for his eyes to adjust to the dimness of the smoke-filled room. The proprietor, a thin, short man, hurried across the taproom, waving to an empty table and set of chairs.

'We prefer a private parlour.' Garrett leveled a look at the man.

'I am sorry, Sir. But there is not a private room to be had. As you can see, the public room is not crowded. Surely this room will accommodate you along with these other fine folk.'

'We will take the other empty table near the window.' Garrett followed Ottley, Joseph, and Samuel to the table as the proprietor scurried back to the kitchen. Shortly, a barmaid returned with four tankards of the establishment's finest ale.

Garrett thought it a pleasure to be seated in a chair and not on the back of a horse. In no time, a plate of mutton, kidney pie, and fresh, baked bread sat before them. Garrett took a bite and his eyes widened at the hot and tasty food. They ate in companionable silence, except for the lewd outburst of three older men who had been drinking more than eating at a nearby table.

'I say. It shan't be long before I have

myself a pretty, young wife and a connection to a noble family,' the gruff sounding man bellowed, slapping one of his fellow table mates on the back.

'You mean you will finally have some lady to take those two daughters off your hands and get them properly married?'

'Just so. She may very well provide me with an heir to boot. And she is quite practical from what I hear.'

'Good quality in a wife. Less likelihood of spending your blunt. You say this here lady is young? Is she older than your girls?'

'Of course she is. At least six years older than my eldest. What are you snickering about Marsden?'

'I'm not snickering. It just seems odd, a young girl wanting to marry an old codger like you.' The third man chuckled.

'I am not a bad-looking man if I say so myself.' The older man framed his face with his hands like an oil portrait.

Garrett could not help but hear the

conversation as he continued to eat. He imagined a small private parlour with a deep chair next to a homey fire. Ah, well.

'Has the young lady clapped eyes on you?' The man addressed as Marsden topped off his tankard of ale.

'No, and I confess Miss Carrington is not privy to the fact that she is marrying me . . . yet.'

Garrett's head shot up at the name. Could this be Miss Carrington's betrothed? No, the man said she didn't know about his plans. It couldn't be Miss Miriah Carrington? Could it? He held his breath and listened.

'Then how come you are so sure she'll have you?' The third man queried the older one.

'Because a young man, who chances to be her brother, has the desire to be a barrister. At present, he is a solicitor. An opening in my firm's inn should occur soon because one of the other barristers is in ill health. Now what do you say to that?' The older fellow grinned from ear to ear.

'Francis!' Garrett spoke under his breath. A pounding began in his temples.

Slanting his gaze toward the other table, Garrett looked the surly man over. He didn't like what he saw. And the old roué was talking about his Miss Carrington. Miriah. His heart pounded in his chest painfully and a cold chill stole over his body.

'Hastings, you are one fortuitous fellow.' The man named Marsden raised his tankard in salute.

Looking across the table at Joseph's unsmiling face, Garrett raised his brows and drew in a deep breath.

'What are you going to do, Gar?' Sitting beside him, Ottley spoke above a whisper.

'The only thing I can do. I am returning to Finchstonbury as soon as possible.'

'Wait till first light. I will return with you.' Ottley glanced over to the other table. The men had ordered another round of drinks.

'We shall all go with you.' Joseph patted Garrett on the shoulder in a show of support.

Samuel shook his head in agreement and added. 'They will not be riding out very soon, I would put a wager on that.'

'Very well, first light then.' Garrett turned his attention back to his plate, though his appetite had disappeared. He kept an ear to the other table for anything else said about his Miss Miriah Carrington. His Miss Miriah Carrington? When had he started thinking of her in those terms? But of course she would be his, soon. First he must return and ask for her hand in marriage.

In no way would he allow her to be used by a man. Especially one old enough to be her father and who wanted her to find husbands for his daughters. As if that were not enough, he wanted her to have his heir. It would be a snowy day in July before he saw

Miriah married to this fellow called Hastings.

Hours later, Garrett tossed and turned in the lumpy bed. The lumps had nothing to do with the thoughts keeping him awake. What if she refused to marry him? Would he tell her about seeing Hastings? With his fists, he pounded the pillow and pulled it over his head. Why couldn't he sleep?

Before dawn, Garrett waited impatiently for Joseph, Samuel, and Ottley below stairs. After looking out the door of the inn, he turned back and started up the narrow stairs only to be met by Ottley coming down.

'I have been waiting on you, Ott.' He barked at his friend. 'Where are the others?'

'They are coming. We knew you were anxious. That is why we got up early. It is still dark out.' Ottley peered out the door as if to prove his point.

The wooden stairs creaked and Garrett glanced up to see Samuel, followed by Joseph. 'May we have something to eat and drink before we depart?' Joseph would be the one to think of food.

'Yes, but make haste, will you?'

The return ride was not one for pleasure, but bent on purpose. Danté seemed to sense his master's urgency and galloped at a steady but swift pace, leaving a thick haze of dust in his wake. Gray clouds hovered above them. The smell of rain wafted on the breeze that slapped Garrett's face.

Joseph said it was divine intervention that brought them into the same inn as Mr. Hastings. Nothing less explained why they happened to overhear his conversation. Garrett contradicted Joseph and said, even though he was not a gambling man, it was pure luck that brought them to that public room. Whatever it was, he was thankful that he happened to be sitting in the taproom at that particular inn at that precise time.

Over the next rise he could see smoke from one of the chimneys of

Finchston Park. Cresting the hill, he pulled up on the reins as Danté pranced in place. The urge to ride straight to Miriah's door was strong. Peering down at his riding attire and his appearance after his long excursion, he thought better of it.

'Come on boy. We're home.' Garrett clicked his tongue and gave Danté his lead. Joseph, Samuel, and Ottley followed close behind.

★ ★ ★

'Brother, what are you doing home? You only departed yesterday.' Abigail peered over Garrett's shoulder at the other men with wide eyes.

'A matter of some import came to my attention. I found that I left unfinished business that cannot wait.' He reached for Abigail's hands and kissed her on the cheek.

'I will have a footman set four more places at the table.'

Later that evening, Garrett gazed

into the fire as a fierce wind blew outside the great house. Wheels turned in his mind while he pondered his next visit with Miriah. Would she be civil to him or offer a cold shoulder like she did at the end of the assembly? Perhaps he should apologize, but that would make him appear guilty. He ran a hand through his hair and leaned his head back against the high-backed chair.

There was nothing for it but that he should simply ride out in the morning and make her an offer in form. Perhaps it would make him seem too eager, but then he was, in a sense, eager. A loud snore coming from the sofa caught his attention. Ottley was lying flat on his back, sleeping. Garrett's eyes burned from the effects of the wind during the long day's ride. Reaching up he rubbed them and a yawn escaped him. A night's sleep in his own bed would do his aching limbs good. With effort, he stood, stretched and strolled over to his friend and shook him. Again he yawned.

'Come on, old man, wake up and go to bed.'

Garrett trudged up the stairs to his suite of rooms. Wind blew the rain against the window. He hoped the deluge would spend itself before morning. It wasn't easy to make calls in the rain. Frowning, he shrugged out of his waistcoat. No sooner had he laid his head down in the pillow than he was asleep.

Sun peeked through a slit in the heavy curtain. Garrett felt refreshed, if one could actually feel such a thing, after a good night's rest. He shaved himself and dressed before his valet came up to the room. A renewed sense of determination soaked into his soul from the sunny new day. The rain had stopped in the night, as he had hoped. Things were going his way.

After sending word to the stable to have Danté saddled, Garrett stepped into the breakfast parlor and indulged in a hearty meal with Ottley.

'Would you be so kind as to

accompany me on a call to the Carringtons? I may need you to distract Miss Carrington while I speak to Miss Miriah Carrington.'

'Of course. Are you planning to invite the ladies on a long walk upon our arrival?' Ottley peered at him across the table and took a bite of toast.

'A walk to the village would be in order, I think. That way, Miss Miriah Carrington shall see how earnest I am at being in her company in front of townsfolk. Perhaps Miss Sneed will see us.'

'I see. You want to ingratiate yourself in Miss Miriah Carrington's eyes.' Ottley smiled and winked. 'Very good show.'

'I chose to do the pretty in all sincerity. Besides, what is wrong with wanting to show her that I wish to be seen in her company?'

'I presume you have the right of it.' Ottley shrugged. 'You do not suppose we are venturing out too early in the day for a call?'

181

'No. This is the country, and I have noticed from a previous call that Miss Miriah Carrington is an early riser. We shall, more likely than not, find her reading or doing needlework. That is, if she is not out-of-doors enjoying the fresh smell after the rain.' Garrett recalled a heady kiss during such a walk. 'I happen to know she enjoys doing just that.'

A short while later, Garrett and Ottley rode quietly up the gravel drive to Greenly House. While talking to Ottley, he looked about for a sign of Miriah strolling around the grounds. Perhaps she had gone into the village already.

The front door opened and a maid greeted them.

'Yes, my lord. Miss Miriah Carrington is in this morning. Follow me, please.'

Garrett breathed a sigh of relief. One obstacle down. His heart raced in his chest and he took a long steady breath to calm his anxiety at seeing Miriah over the impending proposal.

'Lord Rashley and Mr. Ottley, madame.' The servant curtsied and stood back against the morning room door to allow them entrance. Miriah's blue-gray eyes widened considerably as she stood along with her sister and mother. Her father was not in the room. Garrett held her gaze a moment longer before greeting her mother.

'Good morning, Mrs. Carrington.' He bowed and could see Ottley following suit beside him. 'I believe you met Mr. Ottley the other evening at the assembly, did you not?' He waved a hand towards his friend.

'But of course. It is nice to see you again, Mr. Ottley.' A warm smile grew on Mrs. Carrington's features. 'Do take a seat.'

'Thank you, ma'am.' Garrett glanced at Miriah who held her hands primly in front of her. 'I wonder if your daughters would care to join us for a walk to the village? The weather is very fine after the rain.' The pale blue of her muslin dress enhanced the color of her eyes.

The usual gold cross hung on a chain around her slender neck.

'By all means. I am sure the girls would like to take the air. And the exercise shall be good for them after having spent all of yesterday indoors.' Mrs. Carrington looked over at her daughters and waved them out of the room. 'Now hurry along and fetch your bonnets and shawls. Don't keep the gentlemen waiting.'

'Yes, Mama.' Miriah put a hand around her sister's shoulders and led her out of the room. Garrett didn't miss the slanted glance in his direction as she hurried past. The imploring half smile indicated her need to talk to him. She had forgiven him. At least he hoped that was so.

★   ★   ★

Miriah didn't know what to think of the unexpected call. Besides, Lady Rashley had said he had gone away for sporting. Perhaps he changed his mind about the trip. Her eagerness to apologize and show him a kinder face outweighed the reason he returned, whatever it was. She tied her chip bonnet at an angle under her chin and reached for a cream colored shawl from her wardrobe.

Stepping into the hall, she darted to Ann's room and rapped on the door before opening it.

'Make haste, Ann.'

'What will I say to Mr. Ottley?' Ann worried her lower lip.

'You do not have to say a thing. Just listen to his conversation and put in an occasional 'indeed' in the appropriate places. I am sure Mr. Ottley knows you are shy, and he will be happy to carry the conversation. He strikes me as a considerate man.'

'You're beginning to babble, Miriah. And we have not left the house yet,' Ann stepped into her mother's shoes when she was not present.

'Yes, yes, I know. I shall endeavor to keep my tongue still. Come, come.' She rushed Ann part way down the stairs before her sister slowed her by the arm to a stop.

'Miriah. Must we make haste?' Ann admonished.

Miriah pulled a face. She felt so anxious. Something important must have precipitated the visit. She just didn't know what. However, she must not ask. Miriah seized Ann's hand again and urged her to hurry.

Garrett stood when she reentered the parlour. A look of uncertainty flashed in his blue eyes as it had when he first entered, bringing her up short. He hadn't forgotten her manner of incivility when last she saw him three evenings ago.

'Shall we go?' He gestured toward the door and followed her out.

Neither spoke until they had walked a short distance from the house. Ann and Mr. Ottley followed at a discreet pace, she guessed to give her and Lord Rashley a chance to speak privately. Then both began to speak at the same time.

'There is something I . . . '

'My lord, I must . . . '

'Excuse me.' He offered. 'I believe you started to say something?' He turned to look at her.

'Yes.' She felt jittery now that she had his full attention. He couldn't know how flustered she felt when he looked at her so expectantly. Swallowing, she began again. 'Lord Rashley, I behaved badly the other evening. I practically forced you to dance with a lady you appeared not to want to dance with, and then I treated you abominably afterward when you continued to act considerately toward her. It was not the thing for me to do. Please forgive me.'

'Ah.' He turned his gaze to the path in front of them. 'I had the notion you had a change of heart when you saw me lead her out on to the balcony.' He looked back at her. 'Would you believe me if I tell you she complained of being overly warm and looked quite pale? I would not have taken her except she insisted upon it.'

'Ann said as much when I spoke to

her that evening.' A blush covered her cheeks and she lowered her gaze as if to study the path. 'Am I forgiven then?'

'Of course. Why would I not forgive you, Miss Miriah Carrington?' The softness in his voice compelled her to look up into the sincerity she found in his heavenly blue gaze. 'It is my wish that we may become better acquainted over the next fortnight. Please say that it is your wish too?'

She felt her heart beating in her ears. 'I would be honored to know you better, my lord.' Miriah found that she could speak no louder than a whisper. Could he really have a wish to marry her? The thought sent butterflies through her body and she felt she was walking on a cloud at the same time. Was this love? Hope soared in her heart.

His smile brought an immediate softening to his features.

'May I have permission to call you by your Christian name when we are as close to being alone as we are at this moment?'

'Of course, my lord.'

'Garrett.' He corrected her. 'May I hear you say it?'

'Garrett.' She spoke slowly. His smile widened into a grin.

'You speak my name so beautifully, dearest Miriah.'

Giddiness filled her and she laughed lightly. Never could she be happier than at this very moment. It was obvious that he planned to ask for her father's permission to marry her.

A few acquaintances in the village and neighbors nodded their greetings. Miriah offered a polite but abstract response. All she was aware of was that Garrett was walking beside her and talking about the weather, the scenery, and his horse, Danté. She could not get enough of hearing the warmth in his voice as he talked to her. It was as if they were the only two people in the world.

After returning home, Garrett took his leave with the promise that he would return on the morrow to take her up in his curricle. She had never ridden in a sporting vehicle before. Thinking of it made her heart thud in a reckless beat.

That evening, she shared with Ann all that he had said to her.

'Miriah, I believe he is besotted with you.'

'Oh, Ann. Did you feel all fluttery inside when Mr. Sumner spoke to you?'

Ann blushed and looked down at her hands with a half-hidden smile. 'Of course, silly. That was how I knew we were meant to be engaged.'

'It is the most wonderful feeling, is it not?'

'Yes, it is.' Ann spoke in a little voice. 'You will no doubt find it hard to sleep tonight.'

'I do not care if I ever sleep. I want to relive his every word.' She lay back on Ann's bed and sighed.

For the next week, Garrett visited daily. He took her for afternoon rides in his curricle behind matching bays. In the mornings he would accompany her on walks out in the meadow to take in the beauty of the violets and other blooming flowers. They would walk in the shade of the trees where she removed her bonnet only to replace it when they walked out into the sun. Several times he would reach over and tie the bow for her and proclaim it as perfect.

On two different occasions, he took her out to the stream to fish. Ann usually accompanied them, except for the curricle rides when his tiger, the liveried groom, sat behind them for propriety's sake. Mr. Ottley came frequently to make a foursome.

Ann received a letter from Mr. Sumner and became a little more talkative to Mr. Ottley, who like Garrett, did his best to draw her into conversing more easily.

Returning from the last fishing excursion, Miriah stopped short on approaching the house. A strange carriage stood on the front drive.

'I wonder who is visiting? I do not

recognize the carriage.' Miriah glanced over her shoulder to Ann. 'Could this be Mr. Sumner's carriage, Ann?'

'No. I do not recall seeing him ride in such a conveyance before.'

'Perhaps we should be leaving, Miriah.' Garrett glanced at Mr. Ottley as if for his opinion.

'Not until you say your good-byes to Mama and Papa. Please come in with us.' She coaxed Garrett.

'I, for one, would not wish to give the wrong impression if it is Miss Ann's intended.' Mr. Ottley spoke.

'Mr. Sumner knows you have been visiting. I have written him about our duty to Miriah and Lord Rashley.' Ann spoke up uncharacteristically. 'Really. He trusts me wholeheartedly.'

Miriah noticed Garrett studying her sister as if she had grown two heads. What did Ann say to garner such a strange response from him? 'Please come in, Garrett.' Miriah suggested once more.

He glanced back at her with a blank expression, then followed her into the house.

She encountered the housekeeper in the foyer. 'Maybury, who is here?'

'Your brother, Mr. Francis and another gentleman, ma'am.' She curtsied and continued down the hall toward the kitchen.

'Francis? He must have come in his friend's carriage.' Miriah frowned, fearing she knew the identity of the friend, and turned to the closed parlour door. Voices sounded on the other side.

Pushing the door open, she stepped into the room. Francis and a dapper looking older man immediately stood. Their eyes were on her until Ann and the two gentlemen came up behind her.

'Francis?'

'Miriah? What is this?' His gaze went beyond her as did his guest standing beside him.

Her father came forward to make the introductions. In the exchange she noticed Garrett's eyes become as cold as a winter storm when he looked at the older man. She slanted a look at the man introduced as Mr. Hastings. He stared haughtily at Garrett. So this was Francis' friend. A shiver ran down her spine as she took in the man's silver hair. His eyes were as dark and intimidating as midnight. Thank goodness she had talked Garrett into staying awhile longer. His nearness gave her a sense of comfort.

Still, a feeling of tension filled the room. A knife could cut the air. Even the fire from the hearth did nothing to warm the coolness built around them.

'Do have a seat, everyone.' He father appeared poised. Did he feel the strong current, too? She sat on the edge of the sofa with Ann. Sitting near Mr. Ottley, Garrett had not taken his eyes off Mr. Hastings. She wondered if he knew the man and, if so, what had happened between them. The muscles in her neck and back tightened and she wanted to stretch to relieve the tautness. Instead she willed herself to be calm.

Maybury returned with a tea tray. Her mother poured and asked Miriah to pass the tray of cakes.

Mr. Carrington steered the conversation to the weather and crops. Miriah gazed about the room. Grown men stared daggers at one another, like characters in a penny novelette. It would be strangely amusing if it were not uncomfortable. Anger at Francis for foisting this unwanted suitor on her welled up to overflowing. During a lull in the conversation the room was so quiet she thought she could hear a sewing needle drop.

After a few minutes, Garrett and Mr. Ottley stood. The other occupants followed suit.

'We really must be going. Thank you for your hospitality, Mr. Carrington, Mrs. Carrington.' Garrett bowed, then turned to take her hand. 'Miriah. I look forward to seeing you this evening. I shall be by at seven of the clock to transport you to the Thorps' dinner party. Until then.' He raised her hand to his lips and kissed her fingertips. The look in his eyes reflected an emotion she had not seen in them before.

'Until this evening, Garrett.' She smiled at him. It did not occur to her until he had departed the room and she turned around that Francis and Mr. Hastings had heard the exchange between herself and Garrett. For they stood staring at her as if they could see clear through her. She raised her chin a degree and arched her brows.

She had nothing to be ashamed of, but the cold look in their eyes told her they thought she was guilty. Of what, she did not know.

'Girls, I would like your opinions on what I should wear this evening.' Mrs. Carrington rose and ushered Ann and Miriah out of the room. Miriah breathed a sigh of relief when the parlour door closed behind her.

'Thank you, Mama.' She whispered to her mother as they climbed the stairs.

Her mother simply smiled.

A short time later, Miriah heard the grate of wheels and pebbles as the carriage departed the drive. She hoped Francis had not stayed behind, for she certainly did not wish to have a confrontation with him. A feeling deep inside made her believe that he was not at all pleased with her. She did not know why he had an aversion to Garrett, but she knew he did.

7

Garrett stood as the Carrington's parlour door opened. The loveliest creature he had ever seen waltzed into the room. Miriah looked like pure innocence in a cream colored dress with green embroidered leaves along the hem.

His mother had looked just as lovely and innocent. Like his mother, perhaps this woman could fool a man by her outward appearance. Deep inside he knew the opposite sex could be as cold and calculating as the woman who bore him.

Have a care, Garrett, my man. He must shield his heart lest Miriah break it by deserting him after they married. Yet, his pulse quickened at the mere sight of her. Unlike Dorothea, who evoked little, if any, emotion from him.

His gaze met Miriah's as she stepped

closer and the light scent of lavender water drifted toward him. Worry faded to the back of his mind. He smiled. Her blue-gray eyes sparkled in the flickering candlelight from a nearby table. In her hair a dainty ribbon wound its way through curls held back by combs. A few loose strands of hair formed ringlets close to her cheeks. She returned his smile, and he could not deny the attraction he felt.

'Good evening, Miriah.' Bowing, he took the wrap from her maids and placed it about Miriah's shoulders, then offered her his arm.

'Garrett.' Her eyelashes fluttered before she lowered her gaze.

'You are in fine looks this evening.' He whispered close to her ear as he helped her into the carriage. In the soft light of the coach lamp, he noticed a slight blush caress her cheeks.

The other carriage with the elder Carringtons started down the drive as Garrett settled next to Ottley.

'We are pleased that you could join

us, Mr. Ottley. Aren't we, Ann dear?'

Ann smiled briefly before diverting her gaze out the carriage window.

'Your brother is not joining us this evening, Miriah?' Garrett glanced back at the house.

'He departed some time ago and planned to meet us.'

'I see.' How odd that Francis could not wait on his family.

'The Thorps' dinner party should be quite simple compared to the affairs you both are accustomed to attending in London.' Miriah smiled first at Ottley before beaming at him, then added. 'Card games will be played for entertainment after the meal.'

'I assure you that we are quite comfortable at small gatherings.' Garrett glanced at Ottley who acknowledged his agreement with a nod. 'And I find country life soothing to the soul and more conducive to reflection.'

'Truly?'

He smiled at her short response, then added. 'Are you not pleased with the quiet country life?' On one of their first talks, he recalled her pleasure of living in a small community. He wanted to discern if she had a change of heart.

'Of course I am. I had not thought you would be, my lord.' Her gaze didn't waver from his. 'Your answer surprised me, that is all.'

Garrett stole a glance at Ann who caught her sister's attention with a knowing frown. As she resumed her study of the countryside in the twilight, he returned his gaze to Miriah.

She possessed a strong will and a deep faith. Both of which he had come to admire after seeing her handle Francis. Garrett bit his lip to keep from smiling as he thought of her pushing him to dance with Miss Sneed, then becoming jealous. At the time he was confused by her conflicting actions. Now the flattery of her behavior touched him.

They did not see eye to eye on every issue, but he admired her for her candor, none the less. From listening to

Hastings at the inn, Garrett guessed that the man would expect submission from his wife. The man would want to break Miriah's spirit, and Garrett could not in good conscience stand by and allow that to happen.

Since this afternoon it became clear to him that he must ask her permission before addressing her father. Especially, since Mr. Hastings had put in his appearance. Garrett had to make it clear to the older man, and Francis, that Miriah was meant for him.

It was a short ride, not more than twenty minutes. In that time, he could not take his eyes off her. What had transpired after his departure earlier that afternoon? Did she walk outdoors with Mr. Hastings as she had done with him?

Stepping into the grand salon, Garrett tensed, and prickles of annoyance raised the hairs on the back of his neck. The unmistakable brisk voice of Rupert Hastings echoed off the ceiling and walls. Garrett groaned inwardly at the thought of spending an evening in the presence of the odious man. On the other hand, he could view this as an opportunity to see how Miriah acted toward the fellow. *Surely she doesn't look at Hastings the way she looks at me? She can't be like my mother.*

Mr. Thorp, in the person of a short round man, excused himself from a small group of young and matronly ladies. 'Come in. Come in.' He gestured toward the newcomers.

'Good evening.' Garrett bowed to the gentleman. Miriah curtsied and left his side with Ann to visit with Mrs. Thorp and the ladies.

After a short while, the gentlemen took the ladies in to the dining hall where a long table with a bevy of chairs was set up for the dinner party.

Light conversation whirled around them. Garrett leaned toward Miriah, who sat to his right, and whispered. 'I do not think that Mrs. Thorp could have squeezed another chair around the table.'

'I believe you're right, my lord.' She laughed lightly. Firelight from the candelabra reflected in her iridescent eyes.

'It is propitious that you and your sister are petite. I am very fortunate to be sandwiched in between the pair of you.'

'What flummery you indulge in.' Miriah blushed prettily as she looked away.

As he smiled at her, his gaze caught the scowl on Mr. Hastings' face. He obviously didn't like the seating arrangement since he was situated between Mrs. Carrington and an older widow.

Discussion about agriculture, books, and music abounded around the long table as footmen served the turtle soup.

After dinner, the group dispersed to a room set up with card tables.

In the course of the evening, Garrett's gaze often found Miriah's across the room. Never before had he been so keenly aware of a lady's presence. It had to be Mr. Hastings' watchful eye on Miriah that heightened his own interest in her. Once more he reminded himself, marriage was a business matter. The softer feelings added only confusion and hurt. The real issue stemmed from his uncle's will. Yet the churning in his heart belied his rational thinking.

Her actions gave him the confidence that she would accept his suit. The few times Hastings approached Miriah, she spoke briefly to the man in a friendly enough manner. But her look was nothing out of the ordinary, her eyes didn't show the warmth they had when directed at himself.

Before the end of the evening, Garrett singled out his friend to request his aid.

'Ott. Do me a grand favor and escort Miss Ann into the house immediately when we arrive at Greenly. I would like a few moments of privacy with Miriah.'

Thomas looked at him and nodded in understanding. 'Time to do the pretty and ask for her hand, hey?'

Garrett hid his nerves behind a smile. Seeing Hastings in the same room as Miriah put him on edge and compelled him to make his commitment to her known. The more he was in her company, the more he desired to remain near her. Drawing in a slow breath he steadied his emotions. Had this been a crowded ball, he would have delighted in taking Miriah out on a terrace alcove, drawing her into his arms and declaring himself. But a dinner party was not the same as a ball, and it simply was not possible.

In a short while, the party began to disperse. Francis and Hastings took themselves off to Hastings' inn. And true to the plan, upon arriving at Greenly House, Thomas helped Ann down from the carriage and led her toward the portico. Garrett glanced sideways in time to see Ann look back over her shoulder and, just as quickly, she turned her attention to the front door.

'Garrett. Should we not join them in the house?'

Uncertainty flickered across Miriah's features and he wanted nothing more than to pull her into his arms and kiss the doubt away. Instead he forced himself to be rational. 'Yes, but not at the moment. I want a word with you in private.'

Her eyes grew round and she sat even straighter than before, her hands clasped together on her lap. 'As you wish.'

Drawing a breath of the damp night air, he reached over and covered her hands with both of his.

'Miriah. I hope you know how fond I have grown of you since my return to Finchstonbury. Could these feelings be mutual?' He couldn't recall ever being so nervous as he was now. In the faint light her eyes shimmered while a smile quivered on her lips. Slowly, he let out his breath. 'May I have your permission to speak with your father regarding marriage? Nothing would give me greater honor, I assure you.'

'Why . . . ' She hesitated before her response came out in a rushed whisper. 'I would be pleased.'

'May I now have your permission to kiss you?' He didn't ask when he had taken her in his arms before, but he wanted to give her the chance to accept.

The fringe of her lashes cast shadows on her cheeks. Had he not looked down, he would have not heard her affirmative answer. Yet he read it on her lips as she breathed her response. Slowly, he leaned across the space of the carriage and touched her lips with his own. An ember of fire ignited from her soft lips and coursed through his veins to the region of his heart.

★   ★   ★

Miriah beamed as Ann came into her room soon after the carriage rattled down the front drive. 'Ann, I did not think that I could be any happier a

208

week ago, but I am. Garrett is going to speak with Papa tomorrow.'

'How utterly wonderful, Miriah.' Ann hugged her tight. 'I never mentioned this before, but I've noticed a sparkle in his eyes when he gazed at you on several occasions.'

'Did his eyes really sparkle?' Her thoughts lingered on his lips despite her question.

'My, yes. I did not think he was aware of his feelings toward you, though. I am so happy to know that he is, after all.' Ann's voice tinkled with laughter.

Garrett said he was fond of her, and Miriah believed him. Ann's words planted a seed of doubt in Miriah's heart. If he didn't realize his true feelings, then it was up to her to convince him to love her.

A short time later, while staring up into the darkness of her room, Miriah thought of her good fortune. She had assumed that he would ask her to wed him eventually, for he had paid her undue attention since his arrival in Finchstonbury. He even showed remorse after the evening of the assembly where she grew upset with him for taking Miss Sneed outside for air. However, his gaze turned to stone when he encountered Mr. Hastings this evening. What sparked the animosity between the two men? She sighed. Sleep finally came, followed quickly by daylight.

★ ★ ★

'Miss.' The young maid stepped into the room after rapping softly on Miriah's door. 'Your father wishes a word with you after you break your fast. He will await you in his library.' The woman scurried out of the room.

Had Garrett ridden over at such an early hour? If he did, he was very anxious to marry her, indeed. Her heart sang with delight. No longer did she have to dream of a love match, for it had come true with Garrett.

After Sarah helped her into a dress,

210

the maid ran a brush through her hair and pulled it into a chignon.

With light steps, Miriah descended the stairs and hurried into the breakfast parlour. It didn't take long to down a cup of tea. She bubbled in anticipation of the interview with Papa.

Stopping in front of the closed library door, she took several deep, soothing breaths. With a shaking hand she rapped on the door.

'Come in.' She heard her father's deep voice and pulled the door open. A hint of tobacco hung in the air. Calf-bound volumes lined the walls from the ceiling to the floor on opposite sides of the room. This was father's domain, and he was alone.

'You wanted to see me, Papa?' Butterflies danced in her stomach. She walked around the desk and planted a kiss on his forehead.

'Take a seat, my child.'

The strange tone of his voice gave her a feeling of foreboding. She frowned and looked across the desk at him. He was looking down and flicking a piece of lint off the shiny surface of the mahogany top.

'Miriah. I am deeply troubled by a decision I made some two years ago.' When he looked up at her, she could see the anxiety in the harsh lines of his face and the bleak look in his eyes. 'Yet, I cannot in good conscience allow another day to go by without informing you that you are to be a partner in an arranged marriage.'

Her mouth dropped open. A gray haired man with dark eyes came to mind. It suddenly became hard to breath.

'Arranged marriage.' She squeaked. 'W . . . with whom?'

'Lord Rashley.'

Confusion danced in her head. This must be a joke.

She felt as if her breath had been knocked out of her.

'First, hear me out before you pass judgement on either Lord Rashley or myself. Charles Brownhill stipulated in his will that his nephew, Garrett, must marry within a year after his death.'

'So . . . Lord Rashley has chosen me.' She pointed to herself.

'Not quite. Charles chose you for his nephew. As I said, the arrangements were made two years ago. I was a confidante of Charles', yet his request for an arranged marriage between his heir and you took me by surprise. He pointed out the advantages of such a marriage and even convinced me that he thought the two of you were meant for each other. Eventually, I relented and agreed to the match.'

'Papa!' She found her voice. 'How could you? How could he!' Betrayal bounced in her mind from ear to ear and a pounding in her temples clanged along with each beat of her broken heart. How could she believe a word Garrett said about his feelings for her when it was a blatant lie? He had wooed her only for a fortune.

'You would be taken care of hand-somely for the rest of your life. And you would live relatively close to us. Forgive me for wanting what I thought was the best for you.' He stayed her with an upheld hand when she opened her mouth to speak. 'Besides, your mother was losing patience with trying to stifle your incessant talking. Suitors want a docile wife, not one whose chatter drives them away. You are aware of that. Lord Rashley has shown that he can overlook your fault.'

'Papa.' She reeled with astonishment.

'Nay, he has succeeded where your poor mother has failed. We have noticed a difference in your manner of talking since his return. And, might I add, it appears he is most sincere in the attention he pays you.'

Miriah shook her head, unable to accept that view. She saw Garrett in a different light now. He was not sincere in the least and planned to use her. She was not blind to him now.

In a voice whose icy calm she didn't recognize, she said, 'He's paid me attentions only because he wants the inheritance. And I am the means by which he could get it. I am also the reason he shall not have it.' Pushing herself out of the chair, she paced the room and wrung her hands. 'I cannot believe my own father — and mother — agreed to such a scheme against me!'

'Your mother knew nothing about this.'

'You then!' She glared at him as she never had dared before. 'And Lord Rashley! I gave him permission to speak with you today. This cannot be happening to me.' She touched her forehead with her hand. How could she face him after this debacle? Knots formed in her stomach at the thought of seeing the man.

'Now, now, Miriah.' He stood and came around the desk.

'My own father, consigning me like livestock! I cannot believe my ears.' Tears welled in her eyes. Her pulse raced in her temples and she had the urge to run.

'Do not be so hasty to judge either

me or Lord Rashley,' he reasoned.

Miriah groaned. Her fists clenched at her sides. Turning, she raced out of the library, passing a stunned maid before she ran out the back door. She didn't care where she was going. Out-of-doors was preferable to the suffocation of the house.

Tears streamed down her cheeks as she darted across the lawn to a copse of oak trees. The breeze dried salty tears against her face. She ran down a slope leading to the river, then she continued running along the bank.

Stopping, she drew in ragged breaths of fresh clean air and glanced around. Her heart sank. Garrett had fished with her here not three days ago.

She collapsed on the nearest rock formation. Her hands cradled her face as she cried. Hopes of marriage and true happiness were dashed to pieces. Why couldn't he be honest with her? Why couldn't her father have mentioned the arrangement two years ago? Perhaps by now, she would have had time to accept the idea.

Anger, disappointment and trepidation filled her soul. How could Garrett do this to her? He had deceived her into believing that he really cared for her. A spinster's life would be more agreeable than marriage with a man she couldn't trust. The simple truth of the matter was that he intended to use her to gain his inheritance. That hurt more than anything in the world. It was not Christian to hate someone, but it was that emotion that now filled her heart.

* * *

Garrett reined in Danté and took a deep breath. The warm, early summer breeze, mixed with the scent of the horse's lathered coat, steadied his nerves. Having no idea if Mr. Carrington was privy to the stipulation of the will, Garrett was a bit apprehensive about the late morning talk with the older gentleman. Climbing down, he handed Danté over to a waiting servant in front of Greenly House.

The housekeeper led him directly into the smoke filled library. Mr. Carrington was standing, his back to a window, drawing a long draft from his cheroot.

'Good morning, Sir.' Garrett bowed.

Mr. Carrington waved him to a chair. Peering up at the older man, Garrett saw eyes haunted by pain. Miriah's father slumped into a seat behind the desk and laid his cigar on a tray.

'I believe you know the purpose of my visit, Mr. Carrington. Let me first put you at ease. In the past few weeks, I have come to admire your daughter. In fact, I am highly fond of Miriah. So much so, that I shall be very pleased if you would honor me with her hand in marriage.'

Mr. Carrington cleared his throat. 'I must confess to you, that I have expected your declaration since you arrived in Finchstonbury. I also must tell you that I know all about the will and that you must marry Miriah.' His voice was low and Garrett stiffened in

218

response to the lifeless monotone of the older man's words. Did Mr. Carrington see him as an unworthy suitor for his daughter? Perhaps Hastings enticed him with a barrister's position for Francis to sweeten the pot. A dull empty ache gnawed at his soul.

'The inheritance has nothing to do with what I think of Miriah. Let me clear that misconception before we go any farther.' He leveled his gaze at Mr. Carrington, feeling a need to defend himself. 'It is true that, in the beginning, I had no desire to wed at all. But that has changed since I have come to know and admire your daughter.' Garrett bounded out of the chair and began to pace. 'She is a remarkable young lady I would be most proud to call my wife. I would do anything for her and not wish to see her hurt in any way.'

'I see.' Mr. Carrington regarded him skeptically.

Garrett lifted his chin at the challenge he saw in the older man's haggard eyes. 'I also believe that she has an independent spirit that can be harmed by those who wish to bend her to their wills. I cannot, in all honesty, stand by to allow that to happen. In marriage to me, she shall be able to exercise her free will, within reason. The only stipulation I require is that she be a faithful wife and mother, as I shall be a faithful husband and father.' He deliberated whether he should share his feelings regarding trust, or the lack of it. Running his fingers through his hair, he rushed on carelessly. 'If you know anything about my family, you are probably aware that my own mother deserted us when I was a young child. For that reason, I did not wish to marry, ever, for fear that women could not be trusted.'

Mr. Carrington nodded in affirmation while picking up his cheroot and Garrett continued. 'I have noticed a difference in Miriah that sets her apart from the kind of person my mother was. Yet, I will have to learn to trust her.

It is not a part of me, now. I can only say that I have the deepest admiration for her and I feel it is turning into a much stronger emotion. And I shall protect her with my life. You have my solemn word on that, Sir.' His heart pumped spastically, out of sync with the clock ticking from the other side of the room.

'I certainly did not expect you to be so fond of Miriah, as you say.' The older man sighed heavily. 'You must not have realized that I was aware of the circumstance surrounding your uncle's will. In fact, he and I arranged the marriage back then. Though he wanted you to feel that you had the choice of the marriage in order to gain the estate. He didn't want it known as an arranged marriage, simply because of your parents' arrangement. He figured you would balk at that.'

'Why did you not tell me so earlier?' Garrett fell back onto the chair.

'Perhaps I should have. I must tell you that I have had a talk with Miriah this morning. I told her the truth about the will.'

'You what?' Garrett flew out of his chair.

Mr. Carrington splayed his hands and spoke calmly. 'Now, now, She is upset, to say the least. But I cou-'

'Upset! More than likely, she hates me! Why did you feel it necessary to explain the will to her at this late date? Could you not have talked to me about it first? We could have come up with a solution that would not have caused her such . . . such . . . '

'Such pain?' Mr. Carrington finished Garrett's thought.

'Yes. Pain. Where is she? I should go to her and explain it myself.' He started for the door.

'I do not believe this is the time to talk to her.'

Mr. Carrington's words held Garrett as he reached for the doorknob. 'Pray tell, when shall I talk to her if not now?'

'Allow her to get herself under control. If it is any consolation, she is just as angry at me for my part in the arrangement as you.'

Garrett shot a sidelong glance over his shoulder at the frowning man. 'For some reason, I fail to be consoled by your words. I also feel that she will be angrier with me than at you.' There was truth in Mr. Carrington's words. Garrett could imagine her response to her father's revelation and wished he could have done something to squelch the hurt she must be feeling.

'Would you mind waiting until the morrow to talk with her?'

'Yes, I would mind. I prefer to speak with her today. Or at least see her. I cannot leave without explaining myself.' Garrett ran both hands through his hair. She would not have accepted his suit had he told her about the will in the beginning. There was little hope in that. She had to know that he did not intend to hurt her, that he was eventually going to tell her the truth. 'Now tell me where she has gone. I would like to find her and make my peace.'

'She left the room not more than thirty minutes ago. Likely as not, she went to the river to be alone.' Mr. Carrington sighed and slumped lower in his chair.

Garrett bowed and rushed from the library. Stepping out the back door, he took a deep breath and remembered Miriah's favorite spot. She had taken him there when they fished together. As he quickened his pace, he had no idea what he would say, or if she would even allow him to speak to her. But he must see her.

The sound of water trickling over rocks became louder. A footpath through the forest opened up near the water's edge before turning down stream. Finally, around a bend where the brook widened, he saw her leaning against a huge rock outcropping. With her back to him, she looked over the water. Slowly, he walked forward until he was only a few feet away but not close enough to touch her. His heart constricted when she turned a tear stained face to him. Coldness filled her narrowed eyes.

'I do not wish to speak to you, not now nor ever again.' Her voice quavered as she turned away from him.

'Will you not hear me out first?' He watched her push off from the rock and walk farther from him. Following her he went on, 'I did not mean to betray your trust, Miriah. I, of all people, know first hand what that is like. Never would I purposely hurt you. Please believe me. I only want what is best for you.'

'What you really mean is, what is best for you.' She ground out the words over her shoulder. 'And I absolutely refuse to listen to any more of your lies.' Covering her ears with her hands, she stormed away.

His fists clenched and unclenched as he stared at her retreating back. Anger seethed in his chest. Why hadn't her father come to him first? Why did he take it upon himself to explain the will to her? Perhaps Mr. Carrington didn't wish for his daughter to marry him but preferred Mr. Hastings.

A little boy of eight crying his eyes out twenty years ago as he threw a memento of his mother's into the lake flashed through Garrett's mind. He hadn't forgiven his mother: how could he expect Miriah to forgive him? He turned and walked back up the river.

8

Garrett brooded around the house for two days. Reading did little to hold his interest indoors. He vented his frustration by galloping Danté every morning until he was lathered.

Had it only been two days since seeing Miriah? It felt like an eternity to him. There was nothing for it but that he should attempt to see her again. He must clear the air between them. Certainly she would come to see this as a misunderstanding. If she would only listen to reason.

What was he thinking? Her heart took precedence over her mind. He had the feeling this was a lost cause.

By the morning of the third day, Garrett came in from his morning ride, marched up to his room and ordered a bath. He could not put it off any longer. Had he told her about the will in the beginning, she wouldn't have been comfortable getting to know him. He had come to like her and he thought the feeling was mutual until her father revealed all. Miriah had to hear his side of the story.

Standing in front of his pier glass, Garrett chose his waistcoat carefully before he put the finishing touches on the mathematical knot of his cravat. His insides churned from the sudden stab of anxiety in his gut when he stepped out to the stable.

The air felt fresh and clean as he rode toward Miriah's house. Not a cloud marred the pale-blue, June sky. That didn't diminish the doubt that lingered in his head. Surely she would see him. She must. He coaxed Danté with the heel of his boot and turned up the lane, all the while practicing what he would say to her. Being the fine Christian lady he knew her to be, she would relent and hear him out. He would beg her forgiveness. Even go down on one knee if necessary to prove to her that he accepted all blame. That he erred on the part of not knowing her true character. He was deeply grieved for the hurt he heaped on her by his lack of trust in her. If need be, he would explain his deep-seeded mistrust. And he did expect her to listen to him at least before she turned him away.

With thoughts of Miriah filling his mind, he found himself at Greenly Manor in a short time. The servant ushered him into the familiar yellow parlour where he waited, eyes trained on the door. It soon opened. The housekeeper hesitated, took a breath, and spoke.

'Miss Miriah Carrington is indisposed, my lord.' She curtsied and looked straight ahead of her.

Garrett heaved a sigh. 'I shall return on the morrow. If she is indisposed yet again, I shall return the next day, and the next, until she sees me. Please inform her that is my intention.'

'Yes, milord.' She curtsied again, and he walked past her to the door.

Garrett was true to his word. By the end of his brief visit on the third day, frustration taunted him to add. 'Please inform Miss Miriah Carrington, that I shall not leave until I have seen and spoken with her.'

'But my lord . . . '

'I have given you a message to deliver, woman. See that she gets it.' He levelled a look at the housekeeper that sent his own servants scurrying.

'Yes, milord.' Her voice was a monotone as she turned to do his bidding.

Not ten minutes passed before the door swung open. He jumped to his feet at the sight of Miriah. Dark shadows surrounded lifeless blue-gray eyes that held him in contempt. The pain he saw in her bloodshot eyes struck him like a saber from a French-man's bayonet. Her once-softened face appeared to be chiseled out of stone and pale as a sheet. He knew he didn't have much of a chance, but at least she was here in the same room with him.

230

The familiar scent of lavender water touched his nose.

'Please refrain from issuing ultimatums to our housekeeper in future. I will not have it.' Her gaze remained locked into his. 'You have gotten your way. What is it you wish to say to me?'

His heart beat rapidly in his chest. Swallowing, he drew in a deep breath before speaking. 'I came to ask pardon for the hurt I have caused you. I did not mean for that to happen. We've grown comfortable together, enjoyed shared activities. I have grown very fond of you, and I thought that you reciprocated those feelings. You could not say that my kisses meant nothing to you.'

'How dare you speak to me of . . . that! You used me. And being intimate with me in that manner was part of your plan to win me. Well — '

'Madame,' he cut her off, 'the kisses were not planned.' His anger rivalled hers. 'Especially the first one. It was the only way I could keep you from chatting on as you are wont to do.'

The fiery look in her eyes told him he'd heaped more pain on her by telling her the truth. Did she want the sincerity or not? Frustration over what to say and her misunderstanding the matter perplexed him all the more.

'I see.' Her hands clenched into fists at her hips. 'Truth to tell is that my talkative ways irritate you. I must have put you through considerable torture listening to me. But then, your words are always precise and correct. You must think your uncle was wrong in the upper story for wanting you to be leg-shackled to me.'

Her eyes brimmed with tears, but he could do nothing to stop his irrational reaction to her implication that he was without fault and the reference to his beloved uncle. 'You do have a way with words that has no end at times. But I found out how to curb your talk. Perhaps, if you did not speak so incessantly I might have had the opportunity to explain the will myself. I had planned on doing so before long. I didn't want there to be any secrets between us. After my parents' failed marriage I was not about to make the same mistake. My mother walked out on my father — '

'And I can see why, if he used her as you planned to use me!' She interrupted him.

Garrett froze. Slowly, he drew in a deep steadying breath then spoke in a low voice. 'Madame, I do not use people. Nor am I arrogant in my speech, and I did not think my uncle wrong in the upper story. You go too far, too far.' He bowed curtly and brushed past her without another word.

Numbness took over as he strode out of the house and climbed in the saddle. Steering Danté up the drive, he raced for home. She could not know how much her words wounded him. The accusation of using her came back to haunt him. He had been the one charging Dorothea with using him to make another man jealous. Miriah's pained expression pierced his soul. But he deserved it. Nothing he'd spoken came out the way he'd planned. His eyes burned. Crying was a weakness he had not indulged in since his mother left. Yet tears stung his eyes.

How could he have lost control of himself so far as to blame her loose tongue on his inability to tell her about the will? The will. He had not really thought about when he would tell her of it. Yes, he eventually planned to explain it, but he had not thought about precisely when.

Nudging Danté with his heel, he turned him down a bluff and gave him over to a fast-paced gallop. The warm wind brushed his face as he raced to the end of the valley.

An hour later, Garrett returned to the house and gave Danté over to the head groom to be cooled down. He ordered a bath to relieve his knotted muscles. Taking himself off to his room, he pondered his alternatives. Did he have any?

The searing hot water was a balm to

his emotions. He leaned back and closed his eyes. The will stated that he must marry Miriah. No other choice was left to him.

At the beginning, it was true that he had misgivings about the match. And he had to admit that he had used her to gain his inheritance. But seeing the pain he had caused her, and remembering his own resentment towards his mother at her desertion, he knew hiding the truth from Miriah was no better than what his mother had done to him. He felt a difference, but the hurt resulted either way he looked at it.

In the past weeks, he had gotten to know Miriah and had witnessed her strong faith toward others, a faith he now admired. He had come to feel a certain something for her. A fondness for her, as he had told her earlier that day. And he was sure she had feelings for him. If she didn't, her father's revelations and his own lack of wisdom in hiding the truth would not wound her. The thought bruised his heart like a rockslide, jabbing and cutting more the further it plunged. Only her forgiveness would cure it.

But then, he hadn't meant to hide the truth in order to trap her into marriage. He hadn't known her father knew about the will. His uncle's man of business did not lead him to believe anyone outside of his own family knew about the stipulations. He'd never believed he could trap her.

A groan escaped his lips. 'Surely I have ruined any hope of winning her back with my thoughtless words.' Panic like he never knew before welled in his stomach. He would lose her, and he was powerless to stop it.

Of course, she had wounded him gravely by her last statement, blaming his mother's departure on his father's actions and thinking father and son alike. She could not be more wrong. But then she didn't know what really happened.

Pros and cons of what he had to do ran through his throbbing head. The only solution was to try once more to talk with her on a more civil level. He had to stay in control of his temper and show her that he really was sorry for his actions. No matter what the outcome, he did not want her to think him an uncaring, unfeeling man. No, he must explain to her that he knew he had pained her by his omission and, yes, lack of trust.

A short time later, Garrett sat behind his desk. With quill pen in hand, he wrote an imploring request to see her again. He would not force himself into the Carrington's house. No, he would ask permission, as the gentleman he was, and accept her answer.

*   *   *

As the sun warmed the back of Miriah's neck, she sat on the window seat in her room and turned the letter over in her hand. A liveried servant from Finchston Park had delivered the missive from Garrett before breakfast. The man had great fortitude to think she would even accept it. Yet, she did. She studied her name in the masculine script across the front. Miss Miriah Carrington. Her fingertip brushed the inscription, then slipped under the paper near the seal. With effort, it opened.

Finchston Park

My Dear Madam,

I write in hopes I may request your forgiveness once more, and better acquaint you with my reason for not confiding the terms of my dear late uncle's will. It vexes me that your father took it upon himself to do the honors instead of allowing me to explain my true sentiments. Contrary to what you believe, I do have honest and affectionate feelings for you. But first, I must explain my actions.

You are probably not aware of my family background. Let me begin by telling you that I was raised by my father alone from the tender age of eight. You see, my mother took it upon herself to desert us for another man. I have not seen her since that day. I must also humble myself by telling you that I have been betrothed once before. Like my mother, my betrothed ran off with another.

For those reasons, I do hope you understand I harbor a certain sense of distrust in women. I must also admit, since the other lady's betrayal, marriage was the last thought on my mind when I heard my uncle's will. However, seeing you once more and coming to know you has given me a change of heart. Please believe these words echo my honest and sincere feelings toward you and the state of matrimony.

I know not what else to write to you. And please realize had I been raised in a loving family as you, I would not be as cautious in regards to marriage. I beg you to allow me to plead my case in person. I also beg your profound understanding and patience. I have a genuine desire to live with you the rest of my life and will remain faithful to you for all my days. My deepest wish is that, if you choose to marry me, you will remain faithful to me. Nothing else is left to say other than I sincerely wish your forgiveness.

Your obedient servant,
G. R.

Tears blurred her vision. She had hurt him by her comment about his parents. In her heart she knew she must see him again. Miriah reread the letter. No wonder he distrusted women. A feeling of sadness came over her at the betrayal in his past that must lie behind his lack of faith.

Dropping her feet to the wood floor, she padded across to her writing desk and pulled out pen and paper. She wrote a short reply with the request that he visit her that afternoon. Then she found the manservant to deliver the note to Finchston Park.

How could she remain angry with him after he let down his guard and told her of his unhappy past regarding his mother and fiancé? Yet, his deception in pursuing her hurt to the core and filled her with exasperation. Lord, help me find forgiveness in my heart. It certainly would be encouraging if he could show that he trusted me in a small way. Better yet, that I show him that I can be trusted.

Two hours had not passed before hooves kicking pebbles echoed on the front drive. Miriah peered out the window to see Garrett riding up on his chestnut Thoroughbred before she darted back to her mirror for a quick perusal of herself. She patted the curls pulled up on the top of her head and checked her white muslin dress with the woven floral sprigs before turning to leave her room.

The young maid met her in the hall.

'Lord Rashley is here to see you. He is in the yellow parlour, ma'am.'

'Thank you, Sarah.' Miriah drew in a

deep breath. With deliberate steps, she made her way down stairs and turned toward the parlour. She had no idea what she would say to him. In one way, she was ready to forgive him. Yet she mustn't bend to his will so much that he felt he'd done no wrong. It was the same with wanting him to share in her faith. He had to come about in his own way. A little guidance on her part couldn't hurt.

Before stepping in, she dusted her skirt and straightened her shoulders in a show of confidence. Then she pulled the door open.

Garrett stood across the room, facing her. A serious frown marred his face, while he clasped his hands behind his tan riding coat. His golden-brown hair was tousled. She imagined his hands raking through the curls as he waited her arrival. Lines bracketed his eyes and the light blue depths had lost their sparkle as they bore into her. He looked — lonely.

For a brief moment, she wanted to

reach out and touch his cheek and tell him all would be well. But he would jump to the conclusion that she forgave him when she had not totally done so. They must practice honesty between them now.

'Good afternoon, my lord.' She found her voice as she stood rigid waiting for him to answer.

'Miss Miriah Carrington.' He bowed. 'Thank you for reading my letter and allowing me this visit.'

'It was a touching letter.' Walking to a chair near the window, she sat and glanced over at him. His gaze locked into hers and revealed a desolate soul hidden behind the facade of a proud man.

'I am profoundly sorry for the pain I caused you.' He spoke with regret in his deep voice. 'I feared you would reject me if you knew the stipulations of the will.'

'I prefer honesty and straightforwardness. But you do not know me well enough, my lord, to anticipate my reaction to any revelation. I am a very good judge of my own feelings, thank you.'

He placed his hand over his heart, his brows furrowed deeply. 'My sweet, you wound me.'

A knot rose in her throat restricting her voice to a whisper at his endearment. 'And what exactly did you do to me, if not wound?'

'Believe me, I know that I have hurt you. And I beg most sincerely for your forgiveness. I stated the reasons in my letter why I did not tell you. Can you not understand I find it extremely hard to trust a lady to be true and deal honestly with me? After the last incident I vowed never to wed for fear that whoever I married would be like my mother and . . . the other lady. I could not bear it!'

The remorse in his voice filled her with sadness.

'I can forgive what you did because God forgives. And how could I do less? But, I can't marry somebody who doesn't trust me and share with me as a natural extension of trusting God.'

He looked away in a manner of shutting her out. When he said nothing, she searched her mind for a new direction to gain his attention.

'Perhaps the reason you didn't consider telling me about the will is that you are a loner. You don't think to share things with other people. You don't believe you can rely on other people, so you keep things to yourself.'

'That is not wholly true. For I do share deep conversation with my half brother.'

'But not with me. If you want to marry me, you must learn to trust me with more conversation than just the weather.'

'I thought you liked to discuss nature.'

'Yes I do, but I am also interested to hear about your life, the good as well as the not so good. Your father, for instance, was he as bitter as you?' She would understand if his father showed resentment. Perhaps his faith faltered because his father's had.

Garrett strolled to the window and leaned with a hand against the wall. 'At first he was, but later he . . . he seemed to forgive her.' His voice was low and she strained to hear him.

'Then why can you not forgive those who have hurt you?'

He jerked his head around to look at her with intense astonishment on his chiseled features. 'Because what they did was so terrible.'

'What you did wasn't?' A tight laugh escaped her. 'Has it ever occurred to you, that you cannot always be the one to receive, you must forgive . . . others too.' She came close to reciting a verse, but thought better of it.

'You were about to say seventy times seven, weren't you?' His heavenly blue eyes held hers. She swallowed hard.

'Yes.' She breathed.

'I am familiar with the Bible. You will, no doubt, be surprised to hear I have read it from cover to cover under the vicar who was my tutor.' A muscle flinched in his jaw. 'I simply do not believe that God hears our prayers. For He certainly didn't answer mine.'

'Hearing and answering are different matters. You mustn't give up on Him. He does not give up on you. I strongly believe that.'

Garrett looked away as if to hide the raw pain she glimpsed in his eyes. When he turned back, his emotions were schooled.

'I believe it is past time for me to go.'

His words startled her and she frowned. Did he hear anything she said about forgiveness? Or did he shut her out completely?

'If you feel you must, Garrett. I will not detain you.' Holding her apprehensions at bay, she spoke in a calm manner she didn't feel.

She heard him inhale sharply at her use of his Christian name. It surprised her as well. He was momentarily speechless.

Brilliant blue eyes held her gaze to

his when he stepped closer. Finally, he spoke in a low, husky voice. 'All is not lost between us. If you believe He does not give up on me — then you, a lady of deep faith that you profess to be, must not give up on me either. Give me the chance to redeem myself.'

Leaning ever so close, he pressed a warm kiss to her forehead and implored her, 'I am not giving up on us.'

He had listened. And now she watched as he walked out the door.

Oh, Lord. He knows me better than I thought he did. Yet, he must see how his actions have harmed our relationship. Trust is not a subject to be taught. It is a feeling that comes from within one's heart — much like love. How comforting it would be if he could put his trust in me. Then would I hear him say three simple words? I love you. It was foolish of her to think he would say them, but she could still hope that he might come around and learn to trust her one day.

⋆   ⋆   ⋆

Later that night, Garrett laid awake with his hands clasped behind his head on the pillow and recalled his conversation with Miriah. He couldn't forget the disillusionment he saw in her eyes as she talked to him earlier. She forgave him, but chastised him for not forgiving his mother and Dorothea.

'It wasn't as if I hadn't heard much the same words from Joseph.' He murmured into the darkness. The words conjured up thoughts of his father on his deathbed. He spoke of pardoning the woman who'd walked out on him.

'In time, you will forgive her too.' His father whispered. A cold chill had surrounded Garrett's heart at the thought of forgiving his mother. 'God is always with you, remember that, son.'

Miriah said God forgave him. God. Where was God when Dorothea's hasty scribbled note was placed in his hands that fateful day? Where was God when his mother walked out on them?

Garrett rubbed his eyes with his

fingertips. Miriah was different with her deep-seeded faith. To his recollection he had never heard his mother or Dorothea mention their beliefs.

Yet, how could faith be more important than inheritance? Maybe Miriah's head whirled with visions of heaven.

Staring into the darkness, he concentrated on a pair of sky-blue eyes and the memory of bubbling laughter. Pleasant images were more conducive to sleep than cannon fire and war. Recollection of his Christian name on Miriah's lips brought a smile to his own. She couldn't be as angry as she sounded because she'd called him Garrett. Hope filled his heart while he drifted off to sleep with the prospect of tasting her sweet lips in the not too distant future.

9

Miriah gathered red poppies, hare-bells, and maywood out of the side garden. The physical exertion kept her busy from thinking of her last encounter with Garrett yesterday. The warm sun caressed her wounded spirit like a healing balm.

The haunted look on his face swam in front of her again. He was lonely, she was sure of that. In her heart, she sent up a prayer for the little boy who lost his mother.

'Miriah.' Ann came up beside her. 'I dislike seeing you so downcast. You must give Lord Rashley a chance. He needs you to show him the way. He is a good man, after all, and he's taken the time to talk with me. Few men pay me any mind, except for my dearest John.'

Miriah turned around and hugged Ann. 'Yes. Your dearest John. Have you

251

received word from him lately? When is he coming home?'

In the past few days, Miriah had thought of little else than her own problems with Garrett. And here, Ann had not enjoyed the company of her betrothed for three months since his mother's death.

'I received a letter only yesterday.' Ann's eyes beamed and her face flushed with happiness. 'He hopes to be home before Christmas. Then we can be wed.'

'I hope he surprises us all and comes home sooner, for your sake.' Miriah reached up and pushed a lock of Ann's hair under her bonnet.

'Until that time, we must see what can be done for you and Lord Rashley. I have seen the looks he gives you when you are not aware. He is in love with you.'

'I do not think so.' How she wished Ann's words to be true. The look on his features didn't come close to the look of love when last she saw him. It was more a look of anguish and pain.

'But I myself am a lady in love and beloved. I know what adoration looks like in the eyes of a smitten suitor.' Ann smiled wistfully.

'If he loves me, as you say, why would he not trust me and tell me of the will much earlier?' In her heart she held onto the belief that God could break through the most hardened of hearts. Fear was useless, she must rely on faith.

'Perhaps when one has suffered the disappointments that he has with other females in his life, his actions and lack of trust are justified. Put yourself in his place: would you trust a man if you were disillusioned by others of his kind?' Ann's face grew serious. 'Can you not imagine how he feels at being rejected? It must hurt him deeply.'

'I concur with you, Ann. However, I cannot accept his apology. Garrett needs to understand the importance of forgiveness toward his mother and the other lady who are responsible for his mistrust. He blames God for not hearing his prayers. If he had married the other lady, she might have made his life unbearable. In a sense, God may have answered his prayer when she broke her engagement to Garrett. But he hasn't seen her leaving in a favorable light. If that is the case, he has no emotion left in his heart for me.'

A lump grew in her throat almost as fast as the ache in her heart. Saying he would not give up on them didn't prove that he meant it. Greed may have been behind his words, not a deep endearing emotion.

'What shall you do when you see him next, Miriah?'

★ ★ ★

A messenger arrived the next morning as Miriah joined her father at breakfast. The courier delivered an invitation to dinner at Finchston Park for the following evening.

'It appears that Lady Rashley and her sons are visiting. In honour of their stay, the viscount is having a dinner party tomorrow.' Mr. Carrington slanted a look at Miriah. 'Do you wish to attend?'

'Of course, Papa.' Miriah smiled in approval at her father. 'I am no longer vexed with you. Though I must admit my sensibilities were crushed when you explained your dealings with Lord Rashley's uncle to me. You would not have agreed to the terms if you didn't believe we would suit. After all, you did say you wanted what was best for me. And you are far more wise than I am in such matters, and an astute judge of character.'

Within the hour, Ann was in Miriah's room bubbling with excitement as she scanned the close press for the right dress for Miriah to wear to the Finchston Park dinner party.

'You must look your best for him. The lilac sarcenet will bring out your eyes to advantage, don't you think?' Ann pulled the frock out and held it under Miriah's chin for closer inspection. 'This will do nicely.'

'Do you think Garrett and I will have the opportunity for a private conversation with everyone about?' A morning walk would be more conducive to a heart-to-heart chat. Just as quickly, another outdoor stroll came to mind. That one ended in a kiss, actually two. A flush stole up her throat and filled her cheeks with heat at the intimate picture. She forced her thoughts in another direction. 'Why do you suppose Lady Rashley has come to Finchston Park?'

'For a family visit. Why else do you propose she has come?'

'I wonder if Garrett has confided in her about my declining his proposal?' And if he did, would Lady Rashley ridicule her for refusing him? She hoped not.

'That is a possibility. And even though she may want the best for him, she would surely understand your motives in denying him at the time. Perhaps she could offer insight into how you can bring about a change in him.'

'The change will have to come from within him. He will have to make that choice. You can guide a horse to water, but you cannot make him drink.' But she wasn't averse to trying.

After awhile, Miriah strolled out of the front door along the gravel drive and down the grassy knoll. Birds trilled as they fluttered from the Sweet Cicely bush to an oak tree. A breeze lifted the ends of the ribbons holding the chip bonnet to Miriah's head. The question of trust floated in her mind as the clouds moved with the current above.

Trust had never been a problem for her in the past. Her parents were suitable teachers by their fine example. She was fortunate in that respect. In many ways she was grateful for the goodness God had shown her.

Please Lord, show me the way to guide Garrett to You. Touch his heart with love and kindness. Melt the doubt that binds him. Lead me in a way that is helpful. She meandered down a trail by the pond as she prayed.

A twig snapped. Glancing up, she saw Garrett standing in the middle of the path. The gelding's reins dangled from his hand as the horse pulled at the tall grass along the trail. A tentative smile lifted one corner of his mouth.

★ ★ ★

Garrett feasted his eyes on the innocent beauty coming toward him down the grassy path. Even in a day dress of beige, Miriah brightened his morning.

Yet, she didn't have a clue how her amiable good looks, tempered with her regard for others, touched him. Determination to please her overwhelmed him, more so than it had for any other female. Her refusal of his suit had not dampened his admiration for her. Instead it heightened her appeal.

Stopping suddenly, she stared at him with round eyes. After the initial surprise, she found her voice. 'What are you doing here?'

'I came in search of you. Knowing

your penchant for nature, I expected you to be out walking. Do you mind if I join you?' He kept his voice and manner relaxed so as not to bring out the feelings of yesterday. Her easy smile whipped away his doubt.

'Please do.' She came up beside him. The scent of lavender water comforted him as it permeated the air around him. They walked in companionable silence along the water's edge. A cool breeze moved the reeds along the bank.

He wanted to tell her how much he missed her since yesterday. How he longed to be near her and never mince words with her. Perhaps he should start by talking to her about his life as she had mentioned earlier.

'I've been thinking about what you said yesterday. I accept some of the blame for not sharing with you. But as you said, I didn't realize how understanding you might be if I told you the truth. Never have I expressed myself to a lady before, and it does not come comfortably to me to do so now.'

'I appreciate your frankness. And I hope I am not like the other ladies you have been acquainted with. I further feel, there should be no secrets if a man and woman are to deal honestly with one another.'

'What about my lack of belief in God? Do you harbor a resentment toward me because of my lack of faith?' He glanced down at her as she turned her attention to the sky.

'Perhaps if I presented faith to you in a different viewpoint you could see it in a more favorable light. As in nature, one trusts the wind to blow because of God.'

'In that case, God is always around because the wind blows constantly.'

'Another example then, the boat floats because God made it possible.'

'Don't forget. He parted the Red Sea for Moses.'

'Excellent. You understand what I am trying to say.'

'Yes. But I didn't say I didn't believe that there is a God, I simply don't believe that he hears us and answers our prayers.'

'But you mustn't hold on to the past. One must live for today and tomorrow. There is nothing a person can do about what has already been. In future, you can only strive to change for the better.'

'What if I say I am willing to do that for you?'

'When it comes to belief, you must want to change for yourself first. You must forgive others before you can go on with your life. If you don't, the resentment in your heart could destroy you. I don't want that for you.'

Staring into her blue-gray eyes, he glimpsed the emotion in her heart. She wanted him as much as he wanted her, but faith stood in the way. 'You are a very stubborn lady, Miriah.'

'And you are an obstinate man, Garrett.'

'We agree on something. That's good.' His gaze moved to her lips, and he wanted to taste their sweetness. Leaning toward her slowly, he closed his eyes and touched his lips to hers. After a moment, he moved away and gazed into her half-closed eyes.

'I had better leave,' he breathed, afraid to say more and break the spell between them.

Climbing over the saddle, he glanced down at her smiling countenance. Whatever their differences, it didn't matter to him. If a mountain stood in his way, he would move it if she wanted it moved. His need to please her was greater than his need to find fault with those who had hurt him. His very existence depended on her to guide him to what? A better life? The other side of believing?

After leaving the Carrington's property, Garrett recalled what Miriah had said a few days ago, that money and title meant nothing to her if her intended — no, that was not what she had started to say. Wait a moment. She had been about to say 'the man I love.' That was it. Love. Could she really love him?

Staring at nothing in particular, he re-lived the softness of her lips. Never before did a kiss leave him with an overwhelming desire to protect a lady. Her concern for him showed in her sincere manner in which she pleaded with him to forgive his mother and Dorothea. Miriah cared for him enough to forgive him. Caring and forgiveness were the roots to real love.

Garrett pulled Danté to a stop below the hill. Climbing down, he allowed the horse to munch on grass. Garrett ambled toward a tree and leaned back against the knotty trunk and closed his eyes. An ache pierced his heart. How could she possibly love him? His mother didn't. But, then Miriah was not like his mother, or Dorothea. Was there room in her heart for him?

★ ★ ★

Miriah walked to her favorite rock and sat beside the water.

'I shall see Garrett again, tomorrow.' She uttered to herself. All things were possible with God. Yet, she didn't want to fall victim to Garrett's charm if he didn't really love her. The kiss was part of his charm and she didn't want to be drawn into a false sense of hope. He must know her feelings were strong for him, but was he using her still to gain the inheritance? In her heart she wanted to believe that he harbored true feelings for her. But how could she be sure?

Leaning her head back, she offered a prayer for Garrett to forgive his mother and his fickle betrothed. Her own lack of trust was teaching her to understand him. Another prayer winged its way to heaven, for a brighter future for Garrett and her, if God willed it.

Rising, she walked back up the trail to the house. When she crested the hill, she saw Francis conversing with her father under the broad chestnut tree. Catching her eye, Francis stopped talking and looked away. He was not through speaking with Father. Miriah strolled to the house to give them privacy and went up to her room. If Francis was talking to her father regarding Mr. Hastings, she hoped he wasn't trying to convince him that she should marry the barrister. The man was ill mannered and old. Suddenly she recalled the icy exchange between Garrett and Mr. Hastings the evening Garrett requested to speak to her father. She must clear the air with him regarding her lack of feelings toward the barrister, if that was the reason behind Garrett and Mr. Hastings' animosity.

Shortly, she heard her father's voice below stairs. Her interest piqued, she glided down to the study and knocked on the door.

'Enter.'

Stepping in, she looked about to find her father alone. 'Where is Francis?'

'He had to return to London.'

'You mean to say, he came all the way

from London to talk to you?' She frowned. This could bode ill for her.

'A matter arose that he could not let hang in the wind.'

'If the circumstance has to do with Mr. Hastings, I tell you Father, I will not marry the man. He is too old — '

'Of course you will not marry Hastings! I don't want you to marry him.'

She breathed easy at her father's words. 'Thank goodness, Father.'

'If you marry anyone, it must be Lord Rashley. He's a good man, and I believe he will care about you and for you.' He stayed her speech with a stern look. 'I trust you will both resolve your differences and come to your senses.'

'Yes, Father.' How could she tell him that she was striving for a solution to the dilemma with Garrett in her mind and in her heart? What would he say if he knew Garrett had kissed her a short while ago? Being her father, he would have every right to be stern with Garrett for taking liberties with her.

Better he not know of the shared intimacy, or he might insist that they marry as soon as possible. Did she want that? She absently walked out of the room.

10

After dinner at Finchston Park, Miriah watched the animated young boy holding court in the center of the salon. Jacob regaled the small dinner party with his uncle's fishing exploits.

Miriah leaned toward Ann, sitting beside her on the Grecian sofa. 'It is easy to see that he admires his uncle. Garrett has a rapport with them evident by his allowing them to join us this evening.'

'Yes. Lord Rashley isn't averse to holding his youngest nephew on his knee either.' Ann slanted an eye to Miriah, adding, 'He will make a good father.'

'Thank you for your keen observation, Sister.' Miriah flashed an amused grin at Ann. It was clear, Ann favored Garrett as a prospective brother-in-law. Though regret filled her that his lack of faith stood in the way of her accepting him.

A childish laugh drew her attention to the eight-year-old son of Lady Rashley.

'The dragonfly soared away as the rod snapped in two, and Uncle came crashing to the ground. His breath whooshed out of him like this.' The boy's hazel eyes sparkled with glee as he imitated Garrett's actions.

'You forgot to tell that he had to take his boots off and let the mud squish through his toes.' The seven-year-old giggled, only to be reprimanded by the oldest boy standing beside Garrett's chair.

'A gentleman doesn't speak of such things in front of ladies, Jared.' Jonathan puffed up with pride, in a way Miriah had seen Garrett do in the past few weeks. It was obvious he thought himself the man of the family in his father's absence.

Miriah approved Garrett's easy manner around the boys. Just then he reached up and mussed Jonathan's dark blond locks.

'I seem to remember a time when you fell into a pond — on purpose in front of several ladies.' Garrett grinned at his ten-year-old protégé. The boy hung his head, but Miriah could see he was holding in a laugh.

The room buzzed with laughter until Nurse shuffled the lads to their rooms.

'Your sons are a joy, Lady Rashley. Quite handsome young fellows, I might add.' Miriah noticed the look of affection Lady Rashley bestowed on the boys as she bid them a good night.

'Well mannered young men, too,' Mrs. Carrington said with a light-hearted grin. 'By the way, did you receive an invitation from Squire Emberson for the strawberry outing day after the morrow?'

'Of course. I had to talk Garrett into accepting, which took some doing.' Lady Rashley flashed Garrett an exasperated look.

'We always have such fun. The boys

will enjoy it.' Mrs. Carrington beamed.

'They were not invited. Only Garrett and a guest.' Lady Rashley spoke offhand.

Did Garrett prefer fishing with his nephews down by the lake to an adult strawberry party? Miriah certainly wouldn't mind joining Garrett and the boys on a fishing excursion in the near future.

'The squire probably didn't realize your sons were here with you,' Mrs. Carrington offered.

'Not to worry. The boys have their day all planned. They will be content to play on the grounds here at the park.' Lady Rashley turned to Ann. 'Would you mind making up a foursome at cards with us, Miss Carrington?'

'Of course.'

Miriah smiled as Garrett took Ann's place beside her on the sofa.

'Your cook serves an excellent venison roast. Was she your uncle's cook as well?' She asked, waiting for the proper time to share her thoughts on Mr. Hastings.

'Yes, and I am glad to have retained her services. She also has a very good memory of my favorite dishes from when I visited as a youth.' Garrett slanted a look toward the card table before lowering his voice. 'I am fortunate my sister-in-law chose to entertain your parents and Miss Carrington. Surely we can put our time together to more affable use than discussing the hired help.'

'I agree. What do you wish to talk about?' Hope stirred in her breast at the hint, from the gleam in his blue eyes, of an earth shattering revelation.

'My fond admiration for you, Miriah. How can I convince you that we are destined for each other? Please say you will marry me.'

'You are a wonderful person, and I want the very best relationship a man is capable of giving.' She spoke with regret for the love she wanted to share, with a man who wasn't capable of returning the endearment. 'However, until God is in your life, you are only part of a man. You cannot offer me your best if you can't give God your best.'

She didn't know how long it would take for him to understand her, but she was willing to be patient. For now, his crestfallen face touched her with deep sadness.

'I am honestly trying, Miriah, but it doesn't seem logical to me.' He rested his arm along the back of the sofa behind her.

'Logic is not from the heart. A difference between people is more like . . . politics.'

'A subject I understand. You could be a Tory, since I am a Whig, and I wouldn't care. I'd like you anyway.' Sincerity filled his voice.

'This is more basic than politics.' A nervous laugh escaped her as she fought to hold onto her objective. 'You learn to believe because you feel it first with God. More importantly, you can't believe till you trust God.'

'Am I to take this as another rejected proposal?' He furrowed his brow. 'What if I get down on bended knee in front of your family?'

He was teasing her to conceal his hurt. She could glimpse his emotion in the smile that didn't quite reach his eyes.

'Please do not. It would be embarrassing for both of us. I told you I cannot accept your hand until you accept God in your life. Until you can forgive others, you can't understand God's forgiveness.' It hurt her to tell him, but these were her feelings and she had to abide by them.

'I said I will not give up, and I hold fast to my words. I will not give you up to another.' He whispered.

Taking a chance to clear the air regarding the barrister, she forged on. 'I've been meaning to talk to you concerning another matter.'

The line along his jaw tightened. Could he read her thoughts regarding Mr. Hastings? She guessed he did.

'I feel I made a mistake in not coming to you and resolving my lack of feelings for . . . Mr. Hastings. Tell me, was I wrong to think that you harbored a certain resentment toward him?'

He looked at her for a long silent moment. 'I believe it is more disgust than resentment that I feel for him. The man can't appreciate you the way I do. Your brother didn't help the situation. Are you saying I don't have to fret over him stealing you away from me?'

'He is not now, or ever will be a threat. I promise you.' She smiled, hoping to melt the doubt from his stony demeanor.

'I'm very glad to hear that.' He winked.

★   ★   ★

A warm breeze whisked the ends of ribbon holding Miriah's bonnet under her chin. God was listening to her, she could feel it, and see it in the purple wildflowers He painted in patches for her to admire along the lane. Flicking the reins on the pony's rump, she drove the two-wheeled dog cart home from the trek into the village. Ann sat beside her holding their stack of books from the lending library.

Her peaceful mood lasted until she rounded the corner of her father's house. Two men standing beside a carriage turned in her direction.

'What are Francis and Mr. Hastings doing here?' She muttered to Ann. Miriah tightened her hold on the leather straps, causing the pony to toss her head. She slacked off the reins.

'I am sure we are about to find out,' Ann answered with quiet emphasis.

Miriah eyed Francis warily as he approached with a sheepish grin on his face and offered her a hand down.

She glanced at the barrister who stood with his chest protruding like a peacock. His manner wasn't any better today than the last time she cast eyes on the man. Something was definitely afoot. A chill stole up her arms at the offensive way Mr. Hastings had of scrutinizing her from her head to toe in idle fashion.

'I am surprised to see you, brother dear.' Miriah chided herself for allowing sarcasm to creep into her endearment to him.

'I sent Father word to expect us yesterday. He must have neglected to inform you of our arrival.' A light laugh escaped him as he looked about, avoiding her gaze. 'Where have you and Ann been?'

'We made a call on Catherine Hanbury. The three of us went to the lending library to exchange books.' She offered a curt nod to Mr. Hastings before entering the house with Ann. Perhaps the older man was only passing through and not staying.

Unfortunately, he remained to dinner. By the time dessert was served, Miriah's suspicion that Mr. Hastings was staying in the vicinity once more was answered. Francis cut short her long discussion on the newest literary acquisitions in the village to heap more misery on Miriah.

'I am quite sure the lending library

will be in need of an addition, what with all the titles you have brought to my attention.' Francis looked across the table at Mr. Hastings and added, 'By the way, Father says there is to be an outing tomorrow to pick strawberries at the squire's. You must join us. It does a body good to reap nature's harvest after confinement indoors poring over papers for days.'

Miriah froze, her wine goblet poised at her lips. Mr. Hastings at the strawberry picking with her family? What would this do to Garrett's insecurity about her feelings for him?

'Miriah dear, did you find the book I requested from the lending library?' Mrs. Carrington inquired as a servant removed the last serving dishes from the table.

'Yes, Mama.' Miriah eyed her mother curiously, for she had already mentioned that she had procured the particular volume in passing her mother in the hall before dinner.

Mrs. Carrington turned toward Mr.

Hastings, dismissing him, saying, 'We shall see you tomorrow at the outing.'

Following in her mother's wake, Miriah sighed with relief at Mama's easy dismissal of the odious man. She was glad to be out of his sight.

The following morning gray clouds blanketed the sky and the air hung like a damp stocking. Miriah expected rain to fall any minute. The outing to the squire's would surely be canceled.

By the end of breakfast, the sun had come out and burned the clouds away. A wind had picked up, dissipating the humidity. Miriah breathed a sigh of relief. Her spirit soared at another opportunity to spend time with Garrett and further enlighten him with regards to trust. What tactic would he use to convince her to marry him before he found faith this time?

An hour later, Miriah retrieved her wide brimmed, straw bonnet with the blue ribbon that matched her muslin frock.

Stepping below stairs, she cringed

upon hearing Mr. Hastings' gravelly voice coming from the front hall. The sound grated on her nerves. She hoped he wouldn't make a nuisance of himself at the squire's party. If he did, she could be very tactful in ridding herself of unwanted attention from the older man. All she had to do was chatter aimlessly. That is, if this dull ache forming behind her eyes didn't become more of an annoyance.

*　*　*

Garrett squinted. Even his brimmed hat could not shield his eyes from the bright sun that enveloped them in a cover of stifling heat. The earlier breeze had been short-lived.

Taking Jen's elbow, he led her up the grassy slope. An annoying loud voice drew his attention back to the arriving vehicles. The muscles in his back tensed at the sight of Hastings making his way down from his carriage before it stopped rolling, to rush to Miriah's.

The older fellow glanced up to the carriage with a smirk on his face. Garrett groaned, wanting nothing more than to smack it off the man.

'I can see very clearly that I must protect Miriah from the clutches of that old codger.' Sarcasm dripped from his voice as he spoke for Jen's ears only.

'I do believe she would welcome your company over his. As far as I can recall, she had no previous knowledge of her brother and his friend visiting today.'

'Poor girl is chattering on like a buzzing bee.' It concerned him that she was anxious and Hastings was the reason she reverted to her old habit. Then he remembered her long diatribes when he first arrived to see her. Suspicion reared its ugly head. Just two days ago she promised him that Hastings wasn't a threat, now or ever. Did she mean it? Could he trust her?

'Why is she talking in that manner?' Jen inquired.

'Because she is uncomfortable. If I know her,' he tried to convince himself, adding 'and I feel I do, she is purposely jabbering about everything she can think of to annoy the fellow. That is what she is doing.' Please let it be what she is doing.

'Come now. You mean to say she is —'

'Let us get closer and listen.' He interrupted Jen and quickened his pace on the grassy knoll, pulling her along with him. Stopping at a discreet distance, he made a show looking for Jen's parasol in his curricle.

Miriah kept up a constant chatter about the weather today, yesterday and what the farmers hoped for in the coming year. She spoke of the abundance of strawberries and the type of soil suited to them. Come to think of it, she had not stopped talking since she arrived and Hastings attached himself to her side.

After a few minutes Jen spoke softly. 'I see what you mean. He looks positively bored to death.'

'Maybe the gentleman needs rescuing, do you think?' The sooner he could get Hastings away from Miriah the quicker he could discern her feelings, or lack of feelings as she had said earlier regarding the bounder.

'But of course. And you are the one to save him from such boredom.' She teased, pulling her elbow out of his loose hold. 'Leave it to me to cut you a clear path.' She stepped up quickly and touched the older man's arm.

'Mr. Hastings. Does your mother live in Stanford?'

'No. You must be thinking of my aunt.' He smiled at her and without an excuse to Miriah began talking to Jen.

Garrett immediately took Hastings' place and looked deep into Miriah's eyes. He liked what he saw, relief from anxiety. A feeling of ease settled over him and slowed the pounding of his heart. Then she mouthed the words, 'thank you' and reached up to rub her forehead. 'Let us go to that patch of strawberries, shall we?'

He let her lead him away from the

others before he blurted, 'Why is Hastings here?'

She looked him square in the eye, hurt evident on her pale, drawn features. 'I do not know. Why do you not ask Francis?'

He bit the inside of his lip. How could he doubt her candor?

A servant came over and laid a rug on the grass in front of Miriah. Garrett reached for her basket and waited for her to sit and smooth the skirt of her blue dress over her calfskin half-boots. As he leaned to place the basket beside her, she motioned for him to sit with her.

Slowly, he sank to the grass, devising a way to lighten the mood between them.

'I know why Hastings is here. The same reason I am here. You. But then you already knew that.' He watched as uncertainty crept into her expression. Stains of scarlet appeared on her porcelain cheeks and she glanced away. He was moved to say, 'The only difference is, I will do whatever you want. I confess I didn't really wish to come today, but I did because I wanted to be near you. Hastings made you nervous, I saved you. You motioned for me to sit. I complied. How else can I serve you?'

She dropped the strawberry she held into the basket before looking up. There was a pensive shimmer in the shadow of her eyes. 'Have you had a change of heart toward your mother and the other lady? Did you ask God's forgiveness? Has your faith returned to its proper place in your life?'

With three sentences, she knocked the wind out of his sail. When will she ever give up? Drawing in a deep breath it was his turn to look away. She asked the impossible. Suddenly war tactics came to mind, the element of surprise.

'I'll take a chance here.' Looking back into her eyes, he added in a low voice, 'If I promise to climb the moon for you, will you marry me?'

She blinked three times. His heart

soared before she recovered.

'No one can climb the moon.' Astonishment filled her voice, while her expressive face said 'are you mad?'

Somehow he knew she had just sunk his ship. He wasn't backing down. 'It is my way of saying I will do the impossible for you.' They were at an impasse. Determination to win her pushed him onward. 'To prove to you how much I think of you. I am willing to give up the estate and the title. What else do you want from me?' There, he had done it. He couldn't turn back.

Tears welled up in her eyes. He held his breath. Tell me you'll marry me, Miriah. End my misery.

'I . . . I realize the enormity of what you say you are willing to sacrifice for me. And I want to answer, 'yes.' But you know I cannot.' Placing her hand on his arm, she went on. 'I know what you're thinking. That I am a selfish person who wants everything my way or not at all. That simply isn't the case. Faith . . . belief . . . God. They mean a lot to me, as do you. I thought I had explained it clearly, but obviously you don't understand.' Retrieving her hand, she reached up to massage her temples, adding under her breath, 'Oh, my head is at sea, and aching as well.'

His feelings of hurt didn't take away from his concern for her. 'You're as white as a sheet. Are you going to faint? Is there something I can do?' He poised himself to catch her.

'No, I've never fainted in my life. I need to go home. Fetch Papa for me, please.' She closed her eyes and sat very still. 'Do go on, Garrett. I'll be fine as long as I don't move my head.'

Goaded into action he stood and turned, nearly bumping into Francis.

'What is wrong with my sister?' Francis frowned as he peered around Garrett's shoulder. 'What have you done to her, Rashley?'

'Francis, you are vexing me to no end!' Miriah hissed between clenched teeth.

Losing the opportunity to issue a

scathing retort, Garrett raised a defiant brow and spoke in a calmer manner than he felt for Miriah's sake. 'Your sister is feeling ill and wants to be taken home. I'm getting your father.' Looking around, he spotted Mr. Carrington holding his wife's parasol.

'No need.' Francis complied with a half-hearted shrug. 'I will take her home, myself. On second thought, you had better inform my father. I don't have a vehicle. I rode over with Hastings.'

The last thing Garrett wanted was for Hastings to go with Miriah. 'You can take my curricle, if you can handle the ribbons. And don't harm my cattle.' He emphasized. 'I'll borrow a carriage from the squire if I have to. Let me help you get Miriah into the carriage.'

He would have liked to drive Miriah himself, but with her family present propriety wouldn't allow it. Mr. Carrington was the logical choice. But Francis was already here, and Garrett didn't want to come to fisticuffs with

Miriah's brother in public.

Miss Carrington came up beside them as they reached the curricle. 'Miriah, I noticed you looked a bit peaked on the ride over. Do you wish me to accompany you?'

'It isn't necessary. I shall be right as a trivet as soon as I have a lie down.'

'Besides, there's only room for two and I'm the one driving.' Francis puffed up.

Garrett noticed Ann looking toward her father's carriage with a puzzled expression.

'I've offered my vehicle for your brother to drive. It only seats two comfortably, Miss Carrington.'

'I see.' She stepped back.

Garrett held Miriah's elbow with one hand and supported her back with the other, handing her up beside Francis, who held the leather ribbons.

Concern showed in the lines on Miss Carrington's face. 'Be careful, Francis.'

'He will do just fine.' Garrett reassured in words what he didn't feel inside. Until now, he had never seen Francis drive, nor had he heard anyone in the family mention the man's ability with the ribbons. He had better not bring harm to Miriah.

★ ★ ★

'Slow down, Francis.' Miriah held the brim of her straw bonnet over her eyes. The bright sun only served to increase her distress. Garrett's dejected look when she declined to marry him again hadn't helped either. If only he would come to the realization that he must one day forgive those who had hurt him in the past. Honestly, she wanted to shake some sense into the stubborn man.

'I'm not going as fast as you think. It only appears that way from the passenger side.' He kept his gaze on the matching bays, adding, 'How are you feeling?'

'Like the gongs of a hundred long-case clocks are ringing in my head.

My stomach is a little queasy, too.'

'Did your illness come upon you suddenly?'

'No. It began at home, then the pain escalated once I arrived at the squire's. I would have been better off had I stayed home at the first sign of the headache.' She reached up and soothed the pain with her fingertips. 'Why do you ask?'

'It appeared to me that you and Rashley were arguing. I thought — '

'You thought wrong, Francis.' The pounding increased between her temples. If she didn't give him an explanation he would persist until she did, and she preferred he leave her alone. 'I was trying to help him understand . . . trust.'

Miriah wanted to know if Garrett loved her instead of merely thinking of her. If he said he loved her earlier, would she have forgotten every reason she had given not to marry him and accepted his suit? The pounding increased along with the burden of unanswered questions. Still, she thought of another question. What would Francis say if he learned that Garrett had proposed to her, several times? It dawned on her to turn the table on him.

'By the way. Why do you make Mr. Hastings out to be dangling after me, especially in front of Garrett?'

'Oh, its Garrett now, is it?'

She didn't like Francis' obstinate tone. 'I don't wish to brangle with you. Leave off, please.' Glancing ahead, Miriah saw a sharp bend in the road. 'Take that turn carefully now. You haven't answered — oh no!' She grabbed the railing along the back of the seat.

Bursting around the curve, two black horses, lathered from a hard ride, bounded toward them. The driver, stretched to his full height, slapped the reins, urging the animals faster. Miriah couldn't believe her eyes.

'Francis!' She screamed, almost fainting from the jarring pain in her temples.

'Slow your vehicle, you idiot,' Francis yelled. At the same time the highflyer raced past, a second pair of horses darted around the bend pulling a high-perched phaeton and sprinting at breakneck speed down the middle of the road.

Horses neighing and wheels skidding across loose gravel sounded in Miriah's ears. She shrieked at the top of her lungs.

The carriage jostled to one side. Francis jerked the horses first to the right, then the left. One of the driver's horses reared, the other followed suit. Miriah held a death grip on the railing as the curricle bounced and skidded. The blue sky turned to shrubs and grass. Her world suddenly went black.

11

A short while later, a bare back rider slid off the back of a stout black horse. A shiver of apprehension raced up Mr. Carrington's spine at the frowning intruder.

'Is there a Mr. Carrington about?'

Mr. Carrington hurried toward the intruder. 'What is it man?'

'There has been an accident up the road a bit, sir. A young lady has been injured. The gentleman.'

'Miriah!' Mr. Carrington grabbed the man's coat with both hands. 'Is she hurt badly? I must go to her.' His heart pounded in his ears.

'Her eyes were still closed, but she was breathing when I left. They are on the side of the road.' The intruder called out to Mr. Carrington's back as he reached Mrs. Carrington swiftly walking toward him. Ann was close behind her mother.

'What's happened, Mr. Carrington?' Mrs. Carrington's voice shook with fear.

'We must go and see to Miriah.' Turning her about he lead her and Ann quickly to their carriage, the driver alert to the emergency held the carriage door open.

'Someone must send word to Lord Rashley. He left not more than five minutes after Miriah and Francis departed. He must be informed.' Ann insisted.

'Yes, indeed.' Mr. Carrington glanced back at the shocked look of the Squire standing near the carriage. 'Send word to Lord Rashley immediately. Tell him to meet us at our house.'

★　★　★

Several hours later, Garrett jumped off Danté at the Carrington's steps before the horse came to a full stop. His heart beat like a hundred drums leading a charge. He had to see Miriah. She would not have been injured had he not offered Francis his curricle to drive. Garrett felt sure of that.

'Please don't die. Don't let her die, Lord.' He muttered, mindless that he just offered a prayer. Racing to the door, he pounded on it with his fist.

'Milord.' The housekeeper looked at him as if she had seen a ghost.

'Let me in, woman. I must see Miriah.' He barged past her and started for the stairs.

'What is going on, Maybury?' Mr. Carrington called from the top of the stairs, then blinked in surprise. 'Rashley.'

Mr. Carrington started down the stairs. Garrett raced up to meet him, expecting to be turned away.

'I beg you to allow me to see Miriah. It is all my fault. Had I not offered Francis my vehicle, this would have never happened. I have to see her. Please.'

'Now, now.' Mr. Carrington spoke in

a low, soothing voice. 'There is naught you can do. Besides, think of the implication of a man in my single daughter's room.'

Garrett grabbed Mr. Carrington's arms, pleading vehemently. 'I have already lost two ladies who were close to me. If Miriah doesn't wake, I will have lost the third and most important lady in my entire life.'

Heavy footsteps came from up the second floor hall. A graveled voice turned Garrett's insides to granite.

'What's this commotion, Mr. Carrington?' Hastings stared down at Garrett with a thunderous look on his face. 'Oh, it is you, Rashley. I should call you out.'

Francis came from the opposite direction on the landing. 'Could you gentlemen hold your voices down? There is an injured lady lying abed. It will not help her to wake any sooner with all this shouting.'

Mr. Carrington peered back at Hastings. 'This is my house. And I will not allow you to call out anyone, especially Rashley. Is that understood?'

'As you say, this is your house. But you should have a care who enters your home. This jackanapes had no thought to your daughter's safety, foisting his conveyance on them as he did.'

The man was out to discredit Garrett. Garrett started to spring into action when Mr. Carrington held him in a firm grip and shook his head in a tight rejection.

'May I suggest Hastings, that you retreat to your room at the inn and leave my business to me?' Mr. Carrington's voice hardened.

Mr. Carrington dropped his hold on Rashley. Slowly, Hastings descended the stairs and stopped on a level with Garrett. An eternity stretched while Garrett took Hastings' measure. Standing before him, Garrett saw a selfish man, who cared only for what people could do for him. Out of consideration for the Carrington's, and not desiring to be thrown out himself, Garrett refrained from hauling the old codger out.

A clock chimed the hour in a distant room. Drawing a breath, Hastings finally continued down the stairs. The front door opened, then clicked shut on the contemptible man.

'I am not averse to begging. Please, may I see Miriah?' Garrett wasn't past climbing a wall to see her, either. He refrained from sharing that thought with Mr. Carrington.

'It is not proper for you to see Miriah in this fashion.' Mr. Carrington added in consolation, 'but . . . I will allow an exception to ease your suffering.'

Garrett followed the older man and Francis to a room at the far end of the hall. For the first time, he noticed Francis walking with a limp, reminding him of other injuries than Miriah's.

'How did my cattle fare through the accident?' Not once had he thought of his prize bays until now. Miriah was his sole concern.

Francis looked back with indignation

on his brow. 'Your cattle narrowly made it without a scratch. They are retained in our stable for your perusal if you do not believe me.'

'I will see to them after I've seen Miriah.' In a resentful tone he added, 'By the way, you don't look too badly injured.'

'One cannot see my primary injury. Let me assure you that my guilt hurts worse than my leg. It is my fault for not doing more to prevent the accident from happening.'

'The blame isn't solely yours. I must own part of it for lending you the use of my equipage. Had I gone for your father she would have delayed her departure and not met the racers on a curve.' Guilt churned inside Garrett at the idea of bringing injury to her.

At least I am willing to give up my inheritance for her, he reconciled his thoughts. Francis was no better than Hastings, using Miriah to advance his career.

'Blaming yourselves will not help Miriah

recover any better.' Mr. Carrington advised them both. Still, Garrett couldn't separate himself from his own guilt.

Francis nodded but said nothing more as they approached the last room down the passage. Mr. Carrington opened the bedchamber door.

Garrett slowly stepped inside the darkened room. It took a few minutes for his eyes to adjust to the light of a single candle on the bedside table. Mrs. Carrington rose from a rocking chair beside the bed where Miriah lay motionless.

Shock washed over Garrett at seeing Miriah's lifeless form. Fear that he could lose her forever rooted him to the spot. Mr. Carrington's hand came against his back and they quietly moved forward.

Standing next to the bed, Garrett stared at Miriah through a fog of emotion. He blinked his eyes. Reaching down, he touched her cool hand resting on top of the quilt. Cradling her hand in his, he squeezed it gently.

'I am so, so sorry.' Tears fell to the cover as he repeated his words. He would not forgive himself if she did not recover.

'You can't forgive until you can accept God's forgiveness.' Her words cut into his thoughts.

Closing his eyes he bent over her and held her hand up to his chest. Silently he prayed for the first time since he was a child. He berated himself for his lack of trust. Had he trusted her in the first place with the truth about the arranged marriage, she would have accepted him long ago. No she wouldn't, he reasoned. I hadn't learned to forgive back then. But I'm willing to try now.

'Lord, I thought I was in control of my life, but I am not.' His prayer was silent, but fervent. 'I cannot go on without You, or Miriah. Please tell me what to do, Lord.' At that moment, his heart constricted with the pain of never proving to her how much she meant to him and how she had touched him. Most of all, he wanted her to know that he loved her. Miriah couldn't pray to God now. What if he prayed for her? Would God listen to him?

'I am putting my trust in You, God. I pray, do not let me down this time, for Miriah's sake. She mustn't pay for my resentment, my sins. Please, let Miriah wake up.' He opened his eyes and bent down to kiss her hand and placed it under the cover. Then leaning forward, he brushed a kiss on her forehead.

'I love you, Miriah. Don't leave me.' He whispered close to her ear before he straightened and walked out of the room.

* * *

Muffled sounds came to Miriah as if she floated in the sea. Yet her body lay very still. Total darkness surrounded her. She felt only the softness of a feathery cloud.

A deep voice invaded her privacy. 'I am so sorry.'

The melodic baritone was music to

her ears. Of course, she had to be dreaming. Garrett wasn't here. She left him at the strawberry patch.

'I love you, Miriah.'

It was a dream. He would never speak words of love to her.

She imagined a warmth against her cheek. How strange? He could not be that close to her, could he? Why wouldn't her eyes open? She wanted to see if he was really there.

Yet, darkness swallowed her and there was no sound at all. Time stood still.

Voices trickled to the forefront of her mind once more. At first fragments of wispy and hushed sounds broke her solitude. Recognition came with the soft whisper of her mother joined by the deeper mellow voice she heard before.

'Miriah, dear.' A gentle hand touched her forehead. If only she could wake from this deep sleep, she could see her mother's beautiful face.

A hand caressed hers. It felt strong and warm to the touch. Miriah willed her eyes to open. She wanted to tell them she could hear.

Raising her lids just a fraction she managed to see a blurry form through the thickness of her lashes. The shadow of a man with tousled golden-brown hair leaned over her. She tried to speak, but there was a burning sensation in her chest and she couldn't.

'Do not try to talk, Miriah.'

The shadow sounded like Garrett. It was Garrett. Then darkness overcame her once more.

When next she woke, her eyes blinked slowly. A clock ticked somewhere near the bed. The room was dark except for a flickering candle to her right. A chair creaked close by. Her mother's face wavered in front of her in a haze.

'Miriah. Can you hear me?' Her mother took hold of her hand and continued, 'Squeeze my hand if you hear me, dear. The doctor says you have broken ribs and you should not try to talk.'

Miriah tightened her grip.

'Very good, dearest. You must be very thirsty. Let me hold your head so that you may sip.' Her mother placed her hand gently underneath Miriah's head and tilted it at an angle to allow her to drink what tasted like herbal tea and a bitter additive. Before her head fell back on the pillow, Miriah closed her eyes.

Dreams filtered in and out. She heard Garrett's voice again, felt his firm hand on hers.

'Please, my little angel, wake up. It pains me to see you lying so still.'

Miriah forced her eyes to open. His face hovered a breath away. She squeezed his hand. He laughed. With his free hand, he ran his fingers through her hair as it fell over the pillow. Leaning over, he pressed a kiss to her forehead.

'I need you, Miriah, to teach me about forgiveness. I'm trusting you to guide me. Don't leave me.' He planted another kiss on her hand.

'No.' She breathed. If this was a

dream, she did not want it to end. Warm tears slid down her cheeks, trailing to the pillow as she held his gaze. At this moment, she needed him to fill her waking hours with a spring breath of air and to take her for a walk by the pond. She needed the comfort that holding his hand brought her. Endearing words from his lips were a healing balm to her soul.

Her mother shadowed Garrett's shoulder. 'We must let her rest, now.'

Miriah didn't want to rest, she wanted to peer into his heavenly blue eyes the rest of her life. Leaning over, he cradled her hair with his hand and planted a tender kiss on her forehead. Close to her ear, he whispered, 'I love you.' Standing, he replaced her hand on the quilt with tenderness. 'I'll be in the library if you should need me.'

He backed out of the room, his gaze never leaving her until the door closed between them.

★ ★ ★

A week later, Miriah snuggled into a wing chair, closed her eyes and listened to the deep, melodic voice paint a poetic picture from the writings of Samuel Coleridge. The Lake poet's words had never sounded so beautiful to her ears until Garrett read them. Slowly she opened her eyes and studied the smooth plan of his face.

'You read superbly,' she whispered, not wishing to disturb him, yet wanting to express her feelings. Slanting her a look, he winked. Heat blossomed on her cheek. 'Silly man.'

'Would you rather I read Children of the Abbey to you?' He teased. 'You know how I adore a good Gothic romance from time to time.'

Amusement sparkled in his blue eyes; kindness radiated from the attention he lavished on her. His thoughtfulness over the past week had extended to her family. 'It was vastly generous of you to bring a present of two enchanting books for me. And I appreciate your thinking of Ann with the sheet music.

She so enjoys playing the pianoforte. I have a feeling Mr. Sumner will be quite pleased in Ann's improved manner. It is so kind of you to take the time to converse with her. Other men misconstrue her shyness as having nothing of import to talk about. You've given her confidence in herself. For that, I am exceedingly thankful.'

'When one is quiet, it doesn't mean she is not thinking. Nor does it mean she lacks an opinion about what she sees. She just needs encouragement to express what she is thinking. Shyness is one thing, not having a thought in your head is another.'

'Yes, I know what you mean.' She beamed at the happiness she saw in his face at her understanding.

'Now that I am through reciting these prolific poems, what more do you wish me to do for you, my lady? I am most happy and eager to please you.' He gave her his full attention.

It embarrassed her to be granted such power over him. Given the option, she might as well forge on and inquire if he was ready to further his dealings with faith.

'Well,' she started tentatively, remembering he once told her he would climb the moon for her. 'I would like to go to church Sunday, if I am strong enough. And I was wondering if you might go with me. Will you?' She held her breath and watched the tug of war going on in the emotion of his face.

'I . . . am not up to that. It would feel false for me to go, like I had always been a part of the congregation. I would be most uncomfortable.'

How could she make him understand that he was as worthy as anyone in church? That God would welcome him back. He mustn't fear that others would think ill of him. Instead she said, 'It was unfair of me to press you into going against what you feel. God looks into your soul and He can see the goodness that I know is there. What others think does not matter as much as what you feel is right for you to do. No one is going to look down on you for not coming to church before. I think they will be very proud when you choose to join us, but not as proud as I will be.'

She touched a hand to his cheek to comfort the man that she loved more than anything. He must come to God's house in his own time. Then one day soon, she believed he would find forgiveness in his heart for the other two ladies that had hurt him. He hadn't reached that point, yet.

12

An hour later, Garrett sat at his desk. His mind wasn't deciphering figures, but trying to discern the reason Uncle Charles had chosen Miriah to be his wife. Uncle had never married, what did he know of women? However, Uncle had been his confidante and Garrett had bared his soul to him.

A gust of wind blew the curtains away from the tall windows. Pushing away from the desk, he strolled to the French door. Opening it, he stepped out on the walkway leading into the garden. A wren chirped its gay little song. Reminded of Miriah's joy in nature, he smiled at the comfort the fresh scent of blooming flowers mingled with grass brought to him. Miriah would have enlightened him on the weather as a puff of cloud drifted in the wind current above. She was so good to him, for him.

Turning, he walked back to the task on his desk. Still his mind wandered to Uncle's will. Inheritance . . . Miriah. Miriah . . . inheritance? Uncle knew Miriah's character through his association with her family.

'You old reprobate!' Garrett spoke as if to the spirit of his uncle. 'You were matchmaking along with Mr. Carrington. How did you know that we would suit? But you did. Uncle Charles, you bequeathed to me the most prized gift in the world, far greater than this house and estate. Thank you, Uncle, from the bottom of my heart.'

An anvil lifted from his shoulders. Suddenly it didn't hurt that Mother had left; she wasn't his life. Neither was Dorothea. He couldn't even remember what endeared her to him. On second thought, she was the one who approached him. She had manipulated him into thinking he liked her enough to want to marry her. The woman had used him.

Miriah would never do that. No, she wanted him to find peace with himself and God. Adorable Miriah, always so giving, so loving. 'I will do anything for you, sweetest love.'

* * *

'Come, Miriah. You'll feel better for stepping out with us to church today.' Ann prodded her on Sunday morning.

'Yes, I believe it will do me good to see everyone. Besides, I am feeling much stronger. I had mentioned to a friend the other day I might attend if I were up to it.' She'd feel stronger still, if only Garrett would be there. Maybe one day he would accept the hand God offers everyone. She hoped it was so.

Riding in the open landau. Miriah gazed up to the clear blue sky. The sound of birds peeping and chirping as they fluttered from hedge rows were a balm to her soul. She had been cooped up in the house like a hen since the accident.

From the porch of a thatched cottage, sweet jasmine mingled with the vanilla-like scent of wisteria, increasing her pleasure in the outdoors. Happiness was blissful, nothing could make the day better. Except for Garrett beside me.

'Good morning.' Her parents greeted the Smythes, an elderly couple, stepping out of the flowered cottage.

'Fine weather we are having.' Mrs. Smythe smiled broadly.

Sunbeams filled St. Bartholomew's Church through the tall narrow windows of the gray stone structure, dating back to the twelfth century. Ann and Mama sat on either side of Miriah in the family pew.

Just before the service began, she became aware of a whisper going through the congregation. Searching the crowd, she stopped abruptly when her gaze fell on Garrett. He was sitting alone in his uncle's pew. Her heart pounded. He had come to God, and in so doing, he had come to her.

Miriah wanted to go over and sit beside him even though she knew it was not the proper thing for a single lady to do. Besides, the vicar had just laid his Bible on the podium and begun the service.

During the two-hour sermon, she couldn't take her eyes from Garrett. Her thundering heart told her he might disappear if she did. About the time she made up her mind to stop staring, he turned his head slowly until his gaze locked into hers. The hopeful glint in his eyes warmed her from the inside out. She wanted to go to him badly. Instead she smiled and he visibly relaxed and smiled back. A tear found its way down her cheek then another and another, and she finally wiped them away. He winked and turned his head to the front.

For the first time, she was aware of the few people who watched her exchange with Garrett. Heat flooded her face. She looked up at the vicar, trying to listen and compose herself.

316

Still she was bursting with happiness. Surely he was drawn by God's forgiveness to attend.

She prayed, 'I'm sorry I'm not very attentive, Father, but I am so wonderfully happy. Thank you, thank you, thank you, God, for so many things. For blessing me with renewed health, and most importantly for Garrett coming to understand You are here for him too. I am so profoundly thankful. He really loves me.'

By the time the service was over she had found herself staring more at the heavenly-blue eyes across the aisle from her than listening to the vicar's sermon. Ann patted her hand as she followed their parents out of the pew, leaving Miriah seated.

As the rest of the church emptied, her gaze remained transfixed by the man sitting alone until they were the only people left in the building. All the chattering had gone out the front door, leaving the church quiet. Not a sound echoed off the stone walls.

Finally Garrett stood and his steps echoed on the stone floor. Crossing the center aisle, he stood next to her family's pew. He stretched his hand out. Her eyes were still on his as she placed her gloved hand in his. Fire coursed up her arm from his touch. She laughed lightly, joyfully.

'My dearest, lovely Miriah. I told you I would do anything for you.' He spoke with tenderness in his voice. His blue eyes were bright with the same emotion she was feeling. The world stood still. 'Let us walk outside. I wish to hear you expound at great length on the pleasures of spring.'

Easily, he pulled her up beside him with his great strength.

'I didn't expect to see you here. Not that I didn't think to see you later in the day. It is just that you were so adamant yesterday against coming. I am so very delighted you changed your mind.'

'I did a lot of mind and soul searching after I returned home.' He talked as he lead her out the side door, away from parishioners in front of the church. 'I thought of the will, my uncle, and the accident.'

'You were busy.' She laughed nervously, wanting to say more. Instead she listened to him with her heart and mind.

'When I learned you were in an accident, that you were unconscious from hitting your head, I feared you would die.' His voice cracked. 'I couldn't get to you fast enough. Something strange happened along the way. I started to pray. Do you know how long it has been since I prayed? Longer than I care to admit. But I prayed and prayed for you to live. I was afraid I would lose you. I was afraid God wouldn't hear me after years of silence, so I prayed for your sake as well as my own need.'

Speechless with wonder and joy, Miriah felt her lips tremble.

'Finally, you awoke, and I was amazed and thankful. God had indeed heard me and answered my prayers.

Still I continued to pray. I was astonished at the peace I felt from praying. You were right about God having answered my earlier prayers. God knew better than I did what I needed. It wasn't Mother, or Dorothea ... it was you. You are the essence of my being. You are the gorgeous rose blossoming in my soul. You are my spring breath, my winter snow. You are my everything. I can't go on without you.' Tears glistened in his eyes.

Miriah swallowed, unable to hold back her own tears at his moving words. God had answered both their prayers.

'I prayed you'd come back from the Peninsula safely,' she said, tears altering her voice. 'That you would come for me, Garrett. From the moment I saw you at the assembly four years ago and you danced with me. I knew we were meant for each other. I never stopped praying. When you returned to court me, I thought my prayers had been answered. That is, until I learned you were being coerced into marrying me for an inheritance. Then I became angry. I was deeply hurt that you didn't have tender feelings for me. I couldn't bear not to have your love. I'm not practical as much as romantic. But I kept praying you'd come around, and you did. I am so eternally grateful. I love you, Garrett. More than anything on this earth.'

Her heart nearly burst with jubilation as he pressed a kiss to her hand. Joy bubbled in his laugh and shone in his eyes as she squeezed his fingers.

His voice was quiet but deeply sincere as he said. 'My uncle gave me a far better inheritance than the estate by bringing us together

'I don't know what to say.' Salty droplets streamed down her face, and her heart sang with delight.

'I cannot comprehend you being speechless at a time like this. I've come to love the sound of your voice, reassuring me that you're close by. You've even taught me to speak up more. Listen to me, babbling on, and I must admit that I love you for it — for what once annoyed me.' She tried to speak, but he rushed on. 'Yes, I admit it. But now it warms me to hear you. It nurtures my soul. I could listen to you for hours.'

Smiling, Miriah stood on her tiptoes to lay a finger on his lips. 'You're chattering like I once did. And I recall how you silenced me.' Stretching, she bestowed a quick kiss on his mouth.

With a sigh, he gathered her into his arms and kissed her until her bonnet toppled off. Giving her a serious look, he spoke. 'I can come to the point: Miss Miriah Carrington, will you do me the greatest honor in the world, and accept my hand and heart throughout the journey of marriage?'

'Yes, my love. Wherever you go, I will go.'

We do hope that you have enjoyed reading this large print book.

Did you know that all of our titles are available for purchase?

We publish a wide range of high quality large print books including:
Romances, Mysteries, Classics
General Fiction
Non Fiction and Westerns

Special interest titles available in large print are:
The Little Oxford Dictionary
Music Book, Song Book
Hymn Book, Service Book

Also available from us courtesy of Oxford University Press:
Young Readers' Dictionary
(large print edition)
Young Readers' Thesaurus
(large print edition)

For further information or a free brochure, please contact us at:
Ulverscroft Large Print Books Ltd.,
The Green, Bradgate Road, Anstey,
Leicester, LE7 7FU, England.
Tel: (00 44) **0116 236 4325**
Fax: (00 44) **0116 234 0205**

When property developer Connor Grant contracted Natalie Jensen to landscape the grounds of his large country house near Ashley in South Australia, she was ecstatic. But then she discovered he was acquiring — and ripping apart — great swathes of the town. Her own mother's house and the hall where the drama group met were two of his targets. Natalie was desperate to stop Connor's plans — but she also had to fight the powerful attraction flowing between them.

ZABILLET OF THE SNOW

Catherine Darby

For Zabillet, a young peasant girl growing up in the tiny French village of Fromage in the mid-fourteenth century, a respectable marriage is the height of her parents' ambitions for her. But life is changing. Zabillet's love for a handsome shepherd is tested when she is invited to join the La Neige household, where her mistress, Lady Petronella, has plans for her grandson, Benet. And over all broods the horror of the Great Death that claims all whom it touches.

PERILOUS JOURNEY

Caroline Joyce

After the execution of Charles I, Louisa's Royalist father considers it too dangerous for her to stay in England and arranges for her to go to the Isle of Man with Armand de la Tremouille, the nephew of the island's Royalist Governor. Their ship is boarded by Parliamentarians who plan to sail for Ireland, but a storm causes them to be shipwrecked on the Calf of Man. Magnus Stapleton, the Parliamentarian chief, becomes infatuated with Louisa, but she has fallen in love with Armand.

THE GYPSY'S RETURN

Sara Judge

After the death of her cruel father, Amy Keene's stepbrother and step-sister treated her just as badly. Amy had two friends, old Dr. Hilland and the washerwoman, Rosalind, with her fatherless child Becky. When Rosalind falls ill, Amy is entrusted with a letter to be given to Becky on her marriage. When the letter's contents are discovered, it causes Amy both mental and physical suffering and sets the seal of fate upon Rosalind's gypsy friend, Elias Jones.

WEB OF DECEIT

Margaret McDonagh

A good-looking man turned up on Louise's doorstep one day, introducing himself as Daniel Kinsella, an Australian friend of her brother-in-law, Greg. He said he had come to stay whilst he did some research — apparently Greg had written to her about it. Louise's initial reaction was to turn him away, but he was very persuasive. However, she was to discover that Daniel had bluffed his way into her life, and soon she found herself caught up in his dangerous mission.